A FALLEN ANGEL?

A Novel

NIGEL GRUNDEY

A FALLEN ANGEL?
Nigel Grundey

Copyright © 2022 Nigel Grundey
All rights reserved.

ISBN: 9798835641031
Imprint: Independently published

CONTENTS

A FALLEN ANGEL?
FOREWORD

Conventional wisdom has it, every story must have a riveting start to engage the reader; however, I can't promise it with the first chapter. But, be that as it may, it is a 'genuine' beginning; mine! You know: the usual mother and child business, all very mundane. Anyway, bear with me, from then on things changed, for a normal early life led to more exciting teenage years when thought provoking revelations came to light. Unfortunately, the Second World War and occupation had everything in turmoil, while events during it were the cause of circumstances beyond my control in its aftermath and the Cold War.

Admittedly I never wanted a normal existence, my choice being to do something out of the ordinary, yet challenging and fulfilling; however, what transpired was definitely unusual, which by necessity, changed my life completely. As with any human experience, there have been highs, lows and a lot more besides, but nothing that could be considered indifferent.

CHAPTER ONE
'A Child Is Born'
Belgium, 1921

April was the month; the place, a private hospital in the seaside town of Ostend. Where, early one morning a baby girl, soon to be named Marie Angelique, was born to Juliana Legrand and Leon Montagne. There are two anomalies here, for while my parents lived happily together for years, they never did marry. So, how my father managed to convince every authority he came up against, that they were indeed married, I have no idea.

Secondly, in those days, most children were born at home, with the assistance of a midwife; or experienced family members. However, so soon after a pandemic that killed millions; when mother suffered a bad bout of 'flu in her final month of pregnancy, it prompted my father to rush her to hospital, where she remained until a fortnight after the birth.

These events hit my father with an unwanted holiday, which for someone whose very existence relied on him being in the right place at the correct time for work, this sojourn in Ostend could have wrecked his reputation. Despite any misgivings, he stayed by Mother's side throughout, paying the exorbitant fee for her and my nursing; while hiding his biggest disappointment.

Like all fathers he had wanted a son, one he could teach to achieve better things in life; instead, in the years to come, he was confronted with a skinny, wayward female who was probably beyond all understanding.

 Released from hospital, my father now realised his family needed a settled existence, so we journeyed to the south of the country, looking for a safe location. I was later told that the house they chose was a ramshackle building situated on the outskirts of a village, whose inhabitants viewed all incomers with suspicion. However, my memories are of a well maintained, comfortable, but small home surrounded by farmland and woods; the latter a favourite playground for me plus other likeminded local children. Those endless lazy days soon ended, when we were dragged off to school, facing the stern nuns and their ideas on education.
 Obviously, we were accepted by the inhabitants of Berhout by then, for my father's sporadic absences went unquestioned; while mother, when asked, always claimed she didn't know where he went. Oh, come on, Mama, young I may have been, but even then, that sounded like a lame excuse; while making me all the more curious.

CHAPTER TWO
'Awkward Questions'
Berhout, 1929

I suppose it all began, when, at the age of eight, a decision was made to extract the truth from my father about his work. Patently, he wasn't like all the other fathers I knew, most of whom worked locally for six days a week; no, he was around for weeks on end, only to suddenly disappear for varying periods at a time. Annoyingly, I could never discover any rhyme or reason why this should occur; however, it gave plenty of time for the German language lessons Papa insisted on teaching me, saying it may be helpful in the future. Thankfully, languages came easy to me, so within a year I was considered fluent.

With that done, but still determined to find out about Papa's disappearances; on one of our regular walks in a nearby wood, I managed to have him chase me far away from any eavesdroppers. When recovering from our exertions, I broached the question; but the answer was far from satisfactory.

"Papa, where do you go after leaving us?" I began.

"I go to work, Marie," he replied, somewhat hesitantly. "Someone has to provide the money for our food and other necessities, plus your little luxuries."

"Yes, yes, but that's not what all the other fath is it?" I persisted.

"No, because I always have to travel, mee in different places; for my job is spec

secret," he said putting a finger to his lips.
"Why?"
"Because, my girl, it has to be that way! However, one day, I promise to tell you the reason why," his tone indicated some irritation.
"Why can't you tell me now?"
"Because I say so!" he replied sharply. "Enough of this; come on, I'll race you back to the house. First one home gets a chocolate."

If my father thought I would forget about this, he was wrong; despite school and other lessons in life, the pestering was to continue, despite his constant rejections. My desire for the truth had me prowl around our home looking for evidence of what he did. This fruitless search for anything tangible lasted an inordinate length of time, before anything was discovered; though when they were, I had little understanding of what it told me.
The discovery of an unusual key and what it unlocked; showed we had a small collection of differing rifles hidden in the cellar of our house; but I considered it nothing out of the ordinary, for it wasn't unusual for people in rural areas to have guns. Neither did the half burnt, discarded photographs of people, mainly men, tell me anything, for though their names and other details were printed on the reverse, they meant little at the time.

You may think this was remiss of me, but, being educated at a convent school, where strict discipline was enforced and the penalties for transgressions were painful; most of us pupils soon learnt to keep our eyes and ears open, but mouths firmly shut. Speak only when you are spoken to, was the rule, which also applied at home; especially when my mother's intentions for me became clear.

Early in life I was more interested in the rough and tumble of playing with the village boys, rather than being the little lady she preferred. However, as time passed it became clear the intention was to have a daughter with all the attributes to mix in any section of society. The endless lessons on 'correct behaviour' and 'polite conversation' were a bore, while the 'keeping house' routines drove me to distraction.

"Now you are fourteen and capable of child bearing, your education must begin in earnest," announced my mother one day. Oh good Lord, was my first panicky thought, she's not intending to marry me off soon, is she? The prospect of having children and facing endless housebound drudgery had never featured in my admittedly vague dreams for the future! Much to my relief, she continued. "You will learn all about fashion, hairstyles and make up; how to accentuate the positive and cover up the defects."

However, my mother, Juliana, must have been the eternal optimist, for she was looking at a short, skinny, barely forty kilogramme example of young womanhood. Okay, my feminine shape was slowly emerging, but big blue eyes and long fair hair were the only perceivable assets thus far. Sadly, I never would become the petite Marilyn Monroe lookalike she craved; though she never gave up on that quest.

That was but one half of the further education phase; the rest was taught to me by Leon Montagne, my father, who had finally decided I was old enough to understand his unusual career choice.

CHAPTER THREE
'Revelations'
Berhout, 1935

One Sunday, my father and I went on one of our favourite hiking routes to the furthest reaches of the woods, a place considered out of sight and away from any interruptions; where we rested on a fallen tree trunk and gazed at the horizon.

"Marie, you have pestered me for many years about what I do for a living, but, now it's time to reveal all," he suddenly announced. "I am employed to kill other human beings by those willing to pay the price for such a deed. This is something which goes against what your school and the church taught you about morality; plus, it is obviously, illegal."

"What, you just shoot people for a living?" I asked; more intrigued than horrified.

"Not always, as I am sure you have read in the newspapers, there are many ways to kill a person."

"Yes, I realise that," came my reply. "One of our teachers once set the question; why, when accidents, disease and neglect cause enough deaths; do governments employ supposedly intelligent people to develop ever more efficient ways of killing their fellow human beings?"

"Why indeed, but in my case, it was circumstance that brought about the present situation. That is not an excuse, but a cold, hard fact, one I am condemned to live with."

"You will have to explain that to me, Papa," was my request.

With a deep breath, he faced me and explained that after seeing Belgium collapse under the assault of German Armies in nineteen-fourteen, his decision was to flee. Crossing the border into France and immediately joining their Army; his instructors took note of this volunteer's prowess with the rifle. Basic training over and sent on a sniper course, it was passed with flying colours; then he was sent to a front line unit, where after being taken to the trenches, his task was explained to him. It sounded simple; eliminate any officers or other members of the Imperial German Army, who were foolish enough to reveal themselves in his sights.

It turned out Private Montagne was rather good at this, acquiring an unwarranted reputation; being regaled as a sharpshooter who had a heavenly presence looking over him. For reputedly, he killed many enemy soldiers; yet the dead men's compatriots could never react, nor pinpoint his position quickly enough to do anything about it.

The reality of course, was somewhat different, for he did indeed suffer a series of gunshot wounds, especially when transferred to Verdun. This place, which in nineteen-eighteen was suffering yet another of the many battles fought there, was the scene of his last, but life threatening injury. Removed to a field hospital, the wound was dealt with, but his lengthy recovery meant a return to the trenches was delayed until three weeks before the Armistice. Having survived what became known as the Great War and the rejoicing which followed, he was demobilised and sent on his way.

This was when Leon Montagne's life fell apart, for returning to his virtually bankrupt country, Belgium; the ravaged hometown had become little more than a collection of damaged houses, populated by war weary civilians and unemployed ex-soldiers. The flour mill his father and elder brother had worked in for years now lay in ruins; while the survivors neither knew, nor cared, whether the missing family were still alive or dead.

With no trade to speak of and living a hand to mouth existence, he cursed decisions made in the past; his sacrifice and patriotism had served no useful purpose for this present predicament. But, fortunately for his continued health and well-being, help came from an unusual source; for knowledge of those wartime exploits prompted an anonymous person to offer him employment.

CHAPTER FOUR
'More Revelations'
Berhout, Belgium, 1935

Being blackmailed is a never ending and increasing expense; therefore, this unknown victim was willing to pay handsomely to be rid of the perpetrator, despite knowing my half-starved father was in no position to reject any offer. Obviously, he readily agreed; being given the money, a rifle, ammunition and photographs of the target.

The place and time of this deed were left up to him, so, he spent many hours observing the daily routine of this man; eventually deciding the elimination would take place close to the target's secluded house. Unlike wartime, the shooting was straightforward; while to his surprise, he was left untroubled by it. After all, he convinced himself, what difference would another addition make to his already impressive body count?

Nevertheless, with the deed carried out, he acted instinctively and fled to a distant part of the country; where lying low he met my mother, the two of them becoming lovers soon afterwards. Though Papa never realised that word of this contract killing would spread quite so quickly; wiser members of the criminal underworld had already taken note, having a discreet and reliable assassin available for hire was a godsend, should they require that service in the future. It was the start of his long climb to fame, or infamy, depending on your viewpoint; pursued because he soon realised, being a discreet and invisible operator guaranteed a continuous trail of customers willing to pay his fees!

"Wow, Papa, you're a 'hitman', just like the characters in gangster films," I blurted out in awe.

"Correct, but do you really understand what I have told you?"

"Come on, Papa, your little girl isn't a child anymore." I replied crossly. "Hey, all has been revealed, my father is a criminal with homicidal intent! So, how does this work?"

"Firstly, maintain your anonymity and always work alone, it's the only way to stay alive and out of police clutches."

"But, how do prospective customers contact you?" was my obvious question.

"Most targets are normally well known within the criminal fraternity, who, in general conversation, reveal a name and the reasons behind this extreme retribution. If I decide to accept the challenge, the potential customer is given my price by telephone."

"Oh, I see, if they accept and deposit the money in your bank or wherever, the job will be carried out." admiring the simplicity.

"Precisely, young lady," he replied, with a look that suggested his daughter was a little too worldly wise for her age,

"In that case, could you teach me to become the best 'hitman' in the world?" I asked earnestly.

"Pa..pa..pardon!" my startled Papa spluttered. "I will do no such thing! Do you have any idea what it entails to become a contract killer, or what you have to give up? Only the foolhardy and unemployable fall into this game; entering the underbelly of society, where liars, cheats, thieves and murderers, do their worst. Once established, it requires constantly looking over your shoulder to avoid the authorities, or some person seeking revenge; hardly the correct career choice for any right thinking young lady. Besides, your mother would kill me for even suggesting any such thing!"

"Come on, Papa, it's doubtful she'd even notice we had been out training; her every waking hour is filled by the desire for me to become a 'proper' lady, to the point of obsession!"

"Yes, thank you, I am well aware of her grand plans," he concluded.

Leading the way home, a lack of conversation told me Papa was seriously considering my future, plus how to stop me descending into his world; but how wrong could I be?

"You know, I reckon a female contract killer could become the most successful ever," he eventually blurted out. "Think about it, Marie, a well-dressed young lady with a pretty face is welcome anywhere, especially one with good conversational skills. This would allow close inspection of a target, while not alarming them in any way. Another advantage is that virtually every situation is covered, many disguises can be made possible by small changes in fashions, wigs or make up."

"Yes, Papa dear, the same thoughts had occurred to me," said to bring him down a peg or two! Well, that had any more talking falter, with Papa's crestfallen look telling me, he had just unwittingly committed the worst blunder of his life.

CHAPTER FIVE
'Lessons In Life'
Berhout, Belgium, 1935

Papa seemed unsurprised that I had inherited his skill with rifles, because with little instruction from him and the sights adjusted for my left handed style; targets soon had their bulls eyes destroyed. Conversely, there were problems with hand guns, their weight required me to use both hands for a steady aim; let alone counter the recoil. No matter, I persevered until becoming a reasonably good shot; only increased wrist strength, or a lighter weapon would show my true potential.

Noting I was always excited when handling firearms, Papa decided to introduce a different aspect of my training, dragging me outside early one morning, to be confronted with two old fashioned bicycles.

"Why do we have to ride these rusty old things?" I wailed on mounting up, wobbling along in front of him.

"Appearances can be deceptive, because these scruffy, but well maintained bikes are quick and quiet; therefore they are perfectly capable of giving you the element of surprise, or saving your life! Now, follow me and concentrate," he called, on pedalling off at maximum speed along the winding lane; while I trailed behind, trying to keep up. After a while, the fear of falling off lessened, enabling me to ape his every action, as we hurtled round corners, or took on a punishing climb. When a welcome downhill stretch came into view, a furious bout of pedalling had me overtake him, only to come face to face with an oncoming lorry, its load so wide there seemed no space left to squeeze past. It was there I learnt that bicycle brakes are not the best; so, aiming for the only gap available, my eyes were closed as we flashed past to emerge unscathed. My exhilaration was short lived, for some metres further on the right hand pedal dug into the roadside banking; having the bike cartwheel, sending me sprawling in a tangle of arms and legs. Picking his daughter and the bike up, Papa shook his head and said quietly.

"Temper your enthusiasm, my girl! Right, no more racing, let's go home," coming as he dusted me off; then remounted. Honest, I did keep my competitive streak under control from then on; well, nearly always!

Fully focused on my goal of mastering all sorts of firearms, I really was confused when Papa appeared with a motorcycle; why were these important in the great scheme of things?

"Because my dear girl, after your target is eliminated; there will be just a few minutes in which to make yourself scarce. A mastery of all modern transport, this being an excellent example, will increase the chances of leaving the scene fast and blending in with other vehicles," was his honest answer.

So, stuck out in a field some distance from home, I was presented with this small two stroke machine and the following preface to a lecture.

"This is for your own safety, so obey all my instructions to the letter; do we have agreement?" I nodded, to have him point out what the various hand

and foot controls did, emphasizing that smooth operation of these was essential. Having satisfied himself my grasp of the essentials was good enough, he started the engine and we mounted up; to career around the field, complete with him shouting what was going on. Then it was my turn, the first lesson containing more false starts and falling off the machine than anything else. But, it did end with me wobbling around the field, more or less in a semblance of control!

Further lessons had my confidence grow, for Papa soon observed I could now circulate the muddy field at a fair speed, any adverse reaction from the machine being countered with ease.
"Very good," he said encouragingly. "Now we shall consider riding on the roads, a move that requires far more skill and knowledge; for falling off at high speed is always painful and can cause severe injury or death! But, first, an introduction."
I have no idea where this lean and dramatic looking motorcycle suddenly appeared from; but, according to its petrol tank badge, this was a 'red hand' Rudge. Moreover, the sporty design, polished aluminium, shiny black and gold accented paintwork, certainly hinted this machine was no mere runabout. Papa had me sit behind him on the uncomfortable looking pillion seat, before we pottered off down the local lanes.
"Right, hold on tight and lean to the left or right when I do," he shouted as we joined a major road, to increase speed along this smoother surface. The engine note rose and fell as the motorcycle accelerated through the gears, the exhaust's staccato bark morphing into a smooth roar as the machine

went ever faster. With the throttle opened wide, all slower traffic was overtaken and left well behind; until, at last, nothing but empty tarmac lay ahead.

With fair hair all awry and tears torn from my cheeks, I stared into the distance, marvelling as the road appeared to narrow as we plunged into a wooded area; the tunnel of lofty trees and dappled sunlight changing to a green blur, with surreal chinks of brightness guiding us on. A bright speck ahead grew ever larger, before seconds later we burst out into open country, almost blinded by the sudden change.

Lit by sunshine and surrounded by fields of golden corn, Papa had the machine thunder on at undiminished speed; while for some bizarre reason, I attempted to count the endless telegraph poles we passed! This diversion wasn't to last, for the next moment I was thrown forward by heavy braking, as we slowed to turn off the main road, onto a badly maintained lane. We carried on at speed as it snaked its way uphill, around a dizzying number of corners, the tyres scrabbling for grip as we leant over at crazy angles. Reaching the summit, the lane promptly plummeted downhill, heading for a blind corner; where a minor misjudgement had us in the wrong place to negotiate the next one. The heavy braking was of no help, for we still had to slither round the wrong side of a car going in the opposite direction; its driver's muffled shout and shaken fist showing his displeasure. This little upset didn't slow Papa, who continued our ride at a fast and furious pace, hedgerows and trees flashing past at a confusing blur; my heartbeat soaring to an unheard of rate. Then, all of a sudden, the machine braked to a stop and the engine was silenced, with me looking around; belatedly realising we were back where it all started.

"There my girl, that might be needed for a quick escape, could you do it?" he enquired.

"Of course, after the correct training," I replied, still in the throes of high excitement.

"So be it!" Papa declared, kissing me on the forehead.

Said training proved exciting and painful in equal measure, for I learnt not everyone has a heightened sense of balance, or instant reactions; so, they must be learnt. Travelling at high speed on two wheels is as intoxicating as it is demanding; when it all goes wrong, mistakes will be rewarded with grazed elbows, knees or worse. I may have shrugged off the pain, but, oh dear, on seeing the results of this most unladylike pursuit, mother was scathing in her criticism.

To stop the never ending carping from his nearest and dearest, Papa changed tack, deciding his daughter should learn to drive the family's Citroen Light Fifteen car; while well away from home, the motorcycle lessons would also continue.

Fortunately for me, co-ordination of a car's different controls came quickly enough, but, being headstrong and obstinate, I had a thing about speed. The never ending demands to slow down, were to no avail, because, convinced of my invincibility, I blithely continued on. Needless to say, sometimes the lesson didn't end well!

Papa lost count of the minor repairs, which had to be carried out due to my off road excursions; but, when a field gate turned out to be a lot stronger than expected, things changed.

With the car now disabled, courtesy of damaged steering and leaking radiator, not to mention a cracked headlight glass; new rules were enforced, forthwith!

CHAPTER SIX
'Different lessons'
Berhout, Belgium, 1937

Papa's strict rules eventually bore fruit, because I finally learnt that to drive or ride correctly, it required less attention to speed, but more single minded concentration and acquired skill. There was also some praise for my efforts, though it's doubtful he knew how much that meant to me.

The same applied at our forest shooting range, for it became obvious he was alarmed by the now unerring accuracy achieved with all manner of weapons. I could almost read his mind; when would the demand come to take part in a 'hit'?

Mercifully for him, mother delayed this troubling scenario, by whisking their daughter off to Brussels and Paris; the final, but hideously expensive part of my education to become the 'perfect' lady. Having finished school and my mother's extracurricular lessons, it was time for the finishing touches; then to step up and practice what I had been taught!

"You are an attractive and intelligent young lady, my dear," her continual flattery normally fell on deaf ears. "Who has an inbuilt sense of style regarding clothes and make up, so all you have to do is show some pizazz, to have all those young men grovelling at your feet."

At the time, I was unsure why any man would want to do this; but, hey ho, I'd give it a go!

Attendance at the various lessons was mandatory, all of which coerced us into wearing a fixed smile, while being dressed up like overblown fairies; who instinctively knew what to do when confronted by excessive amounts of glass and cutlery on a dining table. For an ordinary person like me, this was bizarre, but then, we also had to totter around on high heels, with books balanced on our heads; while the instructor constantly told us to keep a straight back and exude confidence. Though there was no examination on all of this, if there had been, alas, yours truly would never have passed!

More relevant were the regular evenings out, where I met a surprising mixture of people from different backgrounds and levels of society; being entertained by jovial banter, or enduring stilted conversations. A penchant for not suffering fools gladly, while being circumspect about my father's business, meant learning to converse had to be done by thinking on my feet; not easy, as I found out to my cost.

Yes, some young men did try to court me, though the most handsome and charming of them soon displayed a heightened sense of entitlement, which ignored social skills, or small talk. I played along, listening to their inane flattery and sexual fantasies; though some had to learn that pawing my body would result in a slapped face, while indecent proposals brought forth an excruciating pain in their groins! Retribution was stopped in its tracks, when the men were informed this girl's concerned father had also taught her self-defence; which was no lie!

Papa had considered the slight figure of a daughter needed all the help she could get in the big city. So, while I never entered into a situation where my fingernails or high heeled shoes were needed as weapons, it was good to know they were available if needed!

Though I would never admit to my beloved Papa, that whole dressing up thing and the glamorous surroundings had some appeal; while mixing with differing people, revealed just how much one could learn by just listening to them talk and observing their body language. This new found knowledge was pursued with the upmost vigour from then on.

On returning home and having learnt that the wider world was in a dark phase at that particular time; it was with some trepidation my entry into this scary and unpredictable place was about to take place. But, on reflection, those last few months might just have been the best education yet, considering what was to come.

Unfortunately for the population of Europe, nationalistic rumblings in Germany, Italy and Spain had now changed to outright belligerence and open conflict, casting a dark shadow over everyone's future. All of which meant my entry on the world stage was delayed by my protective parents, while they considered what to do.

Indecision had Papa dithering for far too long; even after the takeover of Austria and Czechoslovakia. Widespread condemnation and veiled threats from other European countries had no effect on the aggressors, whose attentions were now focused on other unfortunates elsewhere.

Despite the increased visibility of new military equipment and personnel around our country, Papa was already convinced that just like in the Great War, Belgium would quickly fall victim to any surprise attack; this belief having him move us, lock, stock and barrel, to France. Confident that this country's well prepared and equipped armed forces would make any enemy think twice about an invasion.

Unfortunately, when German forces moved into Poland and won a speedy victory, doubt crept in; even the declaration of war and the arrival of British forces in Europe, could not dispel his feeling of foreboding. This black mood persisted through the frantic preparations made for our family's survival, the various guns and ammunition being hidden in various places around the new property; along with supplies of tinned food and bottled drink.
Mindful of past privations, part of the large garden was turned over to some locally bought pigs and chickens, while elsewhere, plots were established for the growing of vegetables. If all else failed, there was a considerable sum of money residing in a Swiss bank, where Papa wisely decided to leave it; sure that if the country's neutrality was respected and we all survived the coming conflict, more hard times could be avoided.

After the invasion of Denmark, Norway, Holland and Belgium, said conflict arrived sooner than even Papa thought possible, our area of the Ardennes being occupied hours after the invasion began; France's much vaunted defences rendered obsolete against the 'blitzkrieg' tactics. The first we knew of it, was rumbling gunfire in the distance, closely followed by squadrons of aircraft overhead and an endless number of tanks roaring past the house; though not one fired a shot. The dust had hardly settled before infantry arrived, complete with an array of smaller military hardware, including horse drawn wagons and mounted soldiers. Mother, Papa and I stood in front of our house watching this parade of military might pass by. Our quiet, but sullen reaction of the defeated was probably well known to the invaders, who hardly gave us a second glance. Not that it stopped our worries about what might happen in the future.

These came soon enough, starting with travel restrictions, appropriations and food rationing; witness the hurried search of our property by uncaring soldiers, where the rusty bicycles were ignored, while the motorcycles remained undiscovered. This left just our all too visible Citroen car, which was, of course, commandeered for use as Nazi officer transport.
With Papa's unusual skill being redundant for now and no money coming in, mother, a skilled seamstress, became the family's breadwinner; the reversal of fortunes having my father forever seeking work as a common labourer. Fortunately for me, the young, small female with no mentionable qualifications or skills, meant, luck, or so I thought, had secured a waitress job in the local café.
While my parents buckled down to the new arrangement, it didn't take long for me to discover that satisfying the café owner's carnal desires after hours, was also part of my employment contract. Disappointed by my reaction to this, more so when he attempted to force himself on me; it led to a proper fight. Courtesy of Papa's self-defence teachings, he lost, retreating to lick his wounds. Not only that he received a visit from Papa the very next day, to explain what might happen if this situation arose again.
Surprisingly, I kept the job, which came in useful

when observing any interaction between the occupiers and local people. Adept at spotting drunks, or potential troublemakers before they caused a ruckus, eventually earned me the owner's gratitude. Mind you, it could also have been helped by the arrival of a busty second waitress, one more in need of regular sexual fulfilment. Many a night I left the café after work, to hear the start of squeaking bed springs and moans of ecstasy, both emanating from the owner's upstairs bedroom. Despite this, I started my first romantic encounter during that time, with a local boy, Pierre, who was likeable, but not lovable, especially when he forced himself on me; his behaviour eventually wrecking our relationship.

 So, life went on, an uneasy truce between occupiers and the local population holding firm, despite there being little respect on either side. That is, until the Resistance decided to cause trouble in the local area; their hare brained scheme to disrupt rail traffic on a nearby main line being thwarted by some alert guards. The ensuing gun battle had some of their number killed or injured, while other compatriots slipped away without injury; or, so it was claimed.
 Overnight everything changed, all the village's male population were marched off for interrogation, while every property was searched, then searched again; woe betide any lady or child who objected, for any attempt to stop the task resulted in blows from a well-aimed rifle butt.
 After this reprisal, resentment simmered just below the surface; not only against our occupiers, but the Resistance as well. Their presence in the village was just about tolerated, though they were never forgiven for changing the status quo.

Meaning, while Resistance fighters and the German Army continued to play hide and seek, the rest of the residents just tried to get on with their lives, preferably in peace.

CHAPTER SEVEN
'Love And War'
Ardennes, France, 1941

Sensibly, from then on, the Resistance carried out its destructive events well away from our adopted village, saving it from any more unpleasantness; not that it stopped me from joining their ranks. Okay, for someone whose one desire was to survive this conflict, this was a foolish act; my only defence being, hormones and emotional overload!

When Andre Bergamont first came into the café, my heart skipped a beat; the more I looked at him, the more something drew me to him. There's no explanation of my attraction to this medium height, but badly dressed young man, though his tousled hair, blue eyes and calm demeanour were appealing. Our first words to each other were strictly waitress to customer interchange. However, further meetings, intentional or otherwise, led to us becoming friends, then something more intimate; though it took a lot longer for him to admit what he did in his spare time.

Knowledge of this had me boast of my skill with small arms, proved to him when I 'borrowed' one of the hidden weapons to demonstrate my prowess. Stupid woman, all that did was have me browbeaten by Andre and my ex, his best friend, Pierre, into becoming a fully paid up member of the Resistance; but it also meant I could stay close to my beau. Ignoring all warnings, from my parents and others, we would steal away whenever the night time weather was good, entering the forest for a bit of private canoodling. Stupid to the extreme, for if the Germans or his friends in the Resistance discovered us, there would have been hell to pay; but we did it none the less!

 I couldn't help it, for every time he touched me, there was a warm glow as my nerves crackled with electricity; a sensation never experienced before. Needless to say, it was something that grew more intense when those hands explored more of my body. What with that and the heightened excitement, brought on by doing something extremely dangerous, I would normally return home absolutely fizzing with joy and unable to sleep. As you may have gathered, I was also absolutely and completely in love for the first time; but star-crossed lovers, who were also combatants in a shooting war, are not a happy mix!

 Whenever Andre disappeared, sometimes for weeks on end, I turned into a morose and fretful individual, the pessimist's pessimist! I never discovered whether he had the same reaction when I sloped off to transport the all-important radio from place to place, or even more precarious missions that required an unaccompanied train journey.

 Talking of these little escapades, the dismantled radio parts were transported using Papa's rusty old bicycles and overly large handbags. This was done by females, because the sentries normally let them through checkpoints unhindered; though there may have been an ulterior motive here. Since dress making material was almost unobtainable, mother's redesign of most people's wardrobe had skirt lengths shorten way beyond pre-war norms. So this display of the cyclist's legs, plus an unfounded assertion that French girls were 'easy', may have had lusty young German soldiers eyeing up a potential conquest.

Noting this behaviour, when boarding any train, I would latch on a solo male traveller, staying resolutely to one side and just behind him, when entering or leaving the carriage. The idea of this ploy being; to walk safely past the inevitable railway station checkpoints, by acting as if I were the gentleman's submissive wife or daughter. It worked a few times, but, I was careful never to overdo things.

The rare occasions Andre and I were together on a mission, took place when equipment from England was parachuted down to a predetermined spot. They all required travelling some distance, a danger in itself, to meet with others and set up the light signals in an unknown place; then await the arrival of an aircraft. Most were late, which exposed us to an increased chance of discovery by the Germans, because of the time required to gather up the scattered supplies, load and dispatch a vehicle; or worst of all, transport it away ourselves. We had some aborted flights, misdirected drops and narrow escapes, but, none more hair-raising than the one in April, nineteen-forty-two.

Radio messages around that time, indicated that we were to receive a large amount of explosives, guns and ammunition; parachuted down from two aircraft. They were to be hidden away for use in future diversionary attacks. The wording excited Andre's comrades, for they took it to mean an Allied invasion was imminent; though their elation was tempered by thoughts of where all this equipment could be secreted. Both we and the Germans knew only too well that munitions were being dispatched to the Resistance movement in increasing amounts, forcing them to conduct frequent searches of all potential areas where an arms cache could be located. However, that wasn't our concern; our small group was tasked with guiding the aircraft to a drop point, picking up equipment when it landed, loading it on vehicles and last, but not least, disposing of the parachutes. Andre and I carried substantial knives to help with this process; though whether Mother noticed their absence from her kitchen draw remained unsaid.

This supposedly organised event went wrong from the very beginning, for we arrived late at the selected drop zone; hardly having time to place the signal lamps in position, before two aircraft appeared overhead. The engine noise had barely faded away when their cargo landed with a series of thuds, the sturdy crates strung out along the open field.

Our group rushed out to disconnect the now redundant parachutes, while an ancient lorry chugged quietly across the grass, ready to be loaded. All went well, until its engine stopped and refused to start again; people soon becoming nervous, for any delay meant an increased chance of the Nazis catching us red handed.

Minutes later, a burst of light and the roar of vehicles, closely followed by all too accurate gunfire, realised everyone's fears. A desperate, but unequal fight back took place, in which I played my part, attempting to knock out all lights illuminating the scene. My efforts may have reduced the enemy's advantage a little, but the true ending came when tracer bullets struck one of the crates. Moments later there was an almighty explosion, which lit up the area for a second, showing us a viable escape route, having Andre and I running like the wind for this area of sheltering trees. Partially concealed in the woodland, we slowed to a halt, checking if any pursuers were closing in on us; but it seemed the enemy's attentions were focused on events in the field.

 Hastening away from the scene, we began the trek back to the safety of our village, managing to avoid various checkpoints along the way. Still at the peak of excitement and elated with the safe return to Papa's house, Andre and I embraced, then made love, right there in the garden. In all honesty, it was the biggest thrill of that night!

CHAPTER EIGHT
'Fatal Mistakes'
Ardennes, France, 1943

That one near miss didn't dissuade anyone from continuing the night time activities, but a second escape from certain capture should have had the alarm bells ringing; for it suggested that there was a traitor in our midst. However, buoyed by our previous successes, we blithely carried on; disregarding the presence of S.S. and Gestapo personnel, who had recently joined operations against the Resistance movement.

Our luck ran out one rainy autumn night, when, far from home we prepared to welcome an aircraft carrying not weapons, but a passenger; one who had been sent to co-ordinate future Resistance plans. Unusually, we arrived in good time to set out the lights; then sat around nervously, listening for the aircraft's distinctive drone. It arrived ninety minutes later than promised, by which time we were soaked, cold and fed up; though our reaction was immediate on seeing it approach.

With the lights on it landed safely, where the passenger was removed and hustled away from the aircraft, which immediately trundled off readying for take-off. As it roared away and our lights were extinguished, more illumination appeared, along with the sound of vehicles; having Andre and I subjected to a murderous crossfire moments later. The Nazis had caught us unawares, having quietly bided their time by watching us; their patience rewarded by quickly locating the newly arrived agent, initiating his capture.

 Meanwhile, as the troops attempted to pin us down, their accurate gunfire had found Andre, who suffered a bullet wound to the right arm. After spraying bullets in the enemy's direction, I grabbed his good arm, dragged him upright, then swearing and cajoling at the same time, we ran for our lives. Heading for the only cover I remembered seeing, a hedgerow, all went well until the familiar sound of bullets whining past resulted in his hand slipping from my grasp. Andre fell headfirst into the muddy ground and lay still, as I stopped, turning to see what had happened. Kneeling beside him I felt his head, the hair was wet and sticky, with fragments of something clinging to my hands; then realising a bullet to the back of the skull had killed him.

 My world was torn apart in an instant, but the sound of yet more bullets whining past, had my jumbled emotions overcome by a heightened sense of self-preservation. It urged me on to find cover, so crouching down to present the smallest target, I ran, slipping and sliding across the muddy grass, eventually almost colliding with twigs and branches of my temporary salvation, the hedge!

 Fumbling along till finding a gateway, I slipped to the other side just as the rain stopped and checked my position; escape route confirmed, it had me creep on as quietly as possible, only being brought to a halt on hearing an unusual noise up ahead. A glimmer of moonlight revealed all, dear God, mere metres from me was a German soldier having a pee! Well, hell has no fury like a woman who has just lost the one she loves, so that call of nature was his last; my frenzied stabbing having him slump to the ground, gurgling through a last breath. Elated and appalled at the same time, I ran away, still panting from the exertion, blundering blindly on until total exhaustion overcame me; sinking to the ground and violently retching.

From then on the journey home was fraught, as one lonely and troubled member of the Resistance using every trick in the book to avoid enemy soldiers, who appeared to be everywhere. For, sidling along through a small town, it was pure luck that had me spot two of them emerging from a side street; if it hadn't been for a gang of children, playing nearby, plus some quick thinking I would have surely been stopped and questioned. By joining in their fun, while hoping against hope that my small size and clothing were sufficient disguise; they passed by without so much as a glance.

Much to my parent's relief, their daughter arrived back at the house in one piece, albeit two days later and somewhat dishevelled, not to mention her agitated state of mind. After a bath and something to eat, all was revealed to them; mother being particularly scathing about the antics of the so-called Resistance.

"It's no good complaining, what's done is done," Papa considered. "The major worry is the S.S. reaction and your traitor's report. Mark my words; regardless of any revelations, there is definitely going to be repercussions."

That night, after much tossing and turning, I fell asleep; not realising my life was to be turned inside out once again, in the very near future.

CHAPTER NINE
'Death And regret'
Ardennes, France, 1943

Early the next morning, a drumming on our front door announced the arrival of a S.S. search party, which had me bundled out of the back door and told to run for my life. Just in time, for upon reaching the woods, a group of soldiers rounded the side of the house and scanned the area. The fleeting view of those armed men was enough to have me hastily retreat deeper into the woods; But, insufficiently dressed for the cold and armed only with my purloined kitchen knife; what to do and where to go now?

The café owner was surprised by my sudden appearance at the rear door, more so by the demands for some warm clothing and food.

"Come on, you can charge more for the rolls, while your mistress wears very little anyway, so she won't miss a few clothes," I wheedled.

Helpfully, on eyeing my still blood stained weapon, he didn't argue, so I left with a bag of bread; while wearing a couple of oversized jumpers; the only coat available being useless, as it dragged along the ground when put on my petite frame!

Carefully wending my way through our village, it was hard not to overhear gossiping women discussing results of recent searches, including the shooting of my parents. This had me panic, what had gone wrong, why had it happened, were they alive or dead? Wary of asking questions, my decision was to return home for some answers; not a task to be taken lightly!

By taking a long and circuitous route, I arrived via the woods, to find doors still open and the house unoccupied, but ransacked. Picking my way through the discarded items and smashed furniture, my heart skipped a beat on finding blood stains on the hallway floor, more by the cellar door. About to investigate further, a voice stopped me in tracks.

"Oh, hallo Marie," the sudden greeting had me jump out of my skin. "Calm down, it's only me, Phillipe."

"Do you have to creep around like that; I could have stabbed you," came my anguished retort. "Anyway, do you know what happened this morning?"

"No, not exactly, but it seems that when the soldiers were inside here searching for anything incriminating, they found a rifle in the cellar," he recalled. "Whether it was planted there or not was immaterial, for I was told there was a commotion inside the house; then your parents were dragged outside, ready to be taken away. Their noisy remonstrations of innocence had angered Major Walther, the S.S. officer in charge, who drew his pistol and threatened them; but, despite this, their noisy protests continued, ending when two shots were fired, leaving the accused couple lying on the ground. Ordering his subordinates to place the bodies on their lorry, he was then driven away clutching the contraband weapon."

"Were my parents still alive?" realising this question was a forlorn hope.

"It's too soon to know, others in the Resistance are awaiting any news."

"Did you come here to warn us earlier today?" for I was wondering how he knew so much.

"Yes, but I arrived too late," a downcast Phillipe

replied. "Anyway, you have to make a decision now. It's obvious we have been betrayed, Pierre and the others are gearing up to head west, hopefully avoiding any German search parties, are you coming with us?"

I shrugged my shoulders, unsure of what to do, though the arrival of two more Resistance members; should have had me thinking straight, for they confirmed my parents had died before reaching the German compound. Heartbroken, I burst into tears, incapable of any sensible thoughts, my mind a jumble of grief and despair. In between sobs, Phillipe and Pierre tried again to persuade me to go with them, but vehement refusal had them leave with my parting words.

"Don't worry about me, I'll think of something," said she, not really convinced of anything anymore.

When coherent enough to gather up some necessary clothing, the rest of my rucksack was filled with food and a fully loaded Beretta pistol, which had been hidden away by Papa. Then, taking one of the bicycles, I rode off through the woods to one of Andre's favourite spots, where sat on a fallen tree trunk, emotion overcame me once again. Weeping copiously, an inner rage began to build and the red mist descended; those bastard Nazis had killed the three people I loved more than life itself, so they must pay! First to die would be the officer who came to our house, followed by any one of the scum crossing my path in the future.

CHAPTER TEN
'Revenge And Repercussions'
Ardennes, France, 1943

This unrelenting desire for revenge frightened me in my quieter moments, but that inner voice could not be denied; so a plan was devised. The S.S. officers and their pliant female companions were partial to rowdy drinking parties; therefore, they were no doubt looking forward to the impending New Year celebrations.

Keeping it simple, I intended to get into my target's quarters, carry out the deed, then leave immediately; straightforward, but it relied on help from Major Walther's French lady friend. Firstly, she was to ensure he was intoxicated before she dragged him off to the bedroom; necessary, as I could hardly wrestle with someone considerably larger than myself. Secondly, she was to allow ten minutes to pass before raising the alarm, allowing my escape to go unhindered.

Being in no mood for games, after finding the young lady alone, she was told what to do; along with a warning that any refusal or treachery would also result in her demise. Unsurprisingly, she agreed to my requests.

It was during my careful observations of the entrance to the German officer's quarters that I overheard guards discussing how our local Resistance fighters were arrested; a traitor in their ranks had revealed their hideout. This news had me more determined than ever to succeed, but when it came to the early morning of New Year's Day, there were more guards on duty than before.

Stopped in my tracks, I stood there wondering what to do next; when a lorry arrived at the gate, prompting somebody in the back to begin dishing out bottles! All the guards quickly gulped down their bounty, though I noticed some were already beginning to weave about; obviously this wasn't their first liquid New Year present! The sound of breaking glass from my thrown bottle was distracting enough to allow me to scoot inside the compound undetected, heading for Major Walther's rooms, where an extended period of waiting took place.

About to doze off, I was instantly awake when the drunken S.S. man crashed through the bedroom door, attempting to remove his uniform jacket, only to grunt and collapse face down on the bed; presenting me with my one and only chance.

"This is for my mother and father, you bastard," came as a pillow drowned out the noise of two shots to the back of his head. A slight whimper had me turn to see his lady friend about to run for help, though the sight of my gun had her falter.

"You stupid bitch, come here," had her nervously approach the bed. "I don't like treacherous collaborators." her simpering stopped by a bullet to the heart. Throwing the blood stained pillow away, the victims were forgotten; my immediate concern was now to escape from this enemy compound. It turned out easier than expected, for alcohol had made security the least of any guard's worries; though what reprimand they faced in the morning didn't bear thinking about!

Awakening late that morning in my woodland hideaway, I became aware of heavy equipment moving close by. Rushing to a safe vantage point, I saw small field guns arrive and park near some old farm buildings; meanwhile, more lorries arrived to disgorge troops, who lined up as if on parade. The arrival of a Mercedes staff car, had a group of senior officers alight, look around and discuss something. Coming to an agreement, their leader, a high ranking S.S. man barked out orders at the assembled troops, who then rushed off.

With practised efficiency they rounded up every, man, woman and child in the village, escorting them at gun point to a centuries old barn, close to my hiding place. Everyone was herded inside and the doors locked; further orders having some soldiers arrive with burning torches, who then set light to the building. Despite cold weather, this tinder-box dry structure was soon burning furiously, while screams and pleas for help from those inside were ignored by all, particularly the senior officer, who stood idly by watching the flames. Meanwhile, artillery soldiers received orders to load, aim and fire their big guns, the ear-splitting noise of cannon fire preceded having the village reduced to rubble within seconds; leaving only a pall of smoke and dust hovering over the area. Presumably satisfied with the results, the soldiers packed up and left as quickly as they arrived.

Waiting until the dust had settled, I ventured out to find the whole place unnervingly quiet and devoid of life; for every other living creature appeared to have abandoned the area. Smoke from smouldering remains of the barn still hovered above; bringing with it a nauseating smell of burnt flesh, something you could almost taste. While below, there was just smashed wood, stone and scattered personal debris; oh dear God, my adopted village no longer existed and all the people I had known were dead!

Worse still, all of this was my fault; that all-consuming desire to avenge the deaths of three people had left many more dead and a settlement wiped from the face of the earth. Struggling with the enormity of my crime, I swung between vowing to kill every Nazi whoever lived and frenzied soul searching for a way to atone for my stupidity. Then another worry occurred to me, if there was a traitor within our Resistance group; my name was already known to the S.S. and Gestapo; who would be looking for me by now.

Again, self-preservation overcame all other considerations, having me return to the hideaway, pack up my few possessions and leave in a hurry. With little idea of where to go, my bicycle travels were as random as my black mood of muddled thoughts; a situation which meant human contact wasn't advisable. Luckily for me it was a long, lonely trek, for any unavoidable or chance meeting could very well have proved fatal, for one or both of us. Days passed until hunger began to affect my mood and judgement, desperation leading me to investigate the sight of a vegetable patch situated alongside what looked like a farmhouse. Unfortunately, the path leading to it was rough and slippery after recent rains; this, plus my rundown state, led to me losing control and crashing. I remember the ground coming up to meet me, plus the pain when we met; but no more, as the world went black at that point.

CHAPTER ELEVEN
'Sanctuary And News'
Languedoc, France, 1944

Awoken by a persistent headache, I looked around at this plain room, where only the rug and curtains offered some change from the overall cream colour; however, the faint aroma of lavender coming from my bed's crisp white sheets was appealing. Wondering where this place might be, it soon had me out of the bed and stumbling for the room's only window. The view over open countryside was benign, blue skies and sunshine lit up a wintery scene, with no sign of people. Relief had me turn away, the sight of my knapsack having me rush over and check its contents, the gun and knife, plus clothing were still there, looking untouched. Not sure what to make of all this, the sound of footsteps had me discard it and quickly return to the bed; sitting up as the door opened.

"Ah good, you're awake at last," said the lady bearing a tray. "I've made some soup and bread especially for the occasion, so eat it all up." Placing the tray before me, she watched as I tore the roll apart and devoured my meal, cleaning my plate with a remaining crust.

"My, you must have been ravenous!" she exclaimed, placing the tray on top of a small chest of drawers, the room's only other furniture. "Now, Marie, would you care to explain why you have ended up so far from home?"

"Never mind that, where am I and who are you?" came the demand.

"My name is Celeste and this is my house, so have no fear, you are safe," she softly assured me. "Take things easy, we have to make sure these injuries heal," pointing to my head.

"How do you know my name?" I asked, eyeing the plainly dressed, but still attractive woman, who I guessed was in her thirties. She merely smiled, taking a familiar looking paper from her apron pocket.

"This is yours, I hope?" receiving a nod after reading it. "That being so, my guess is you are a member of the Resistance, who has travelled south to avoid arrest because our occupiers don't like what your group have been up to. If this is true, please don't tell me the gory details, what I don't know can't lead to trouble."

"You're correct, so what happens now?" I enquired.

"Hopefully nothing; my act of portraying the grieving widow has been so convincing that the Nazis, nor their Militia friends, even bother me now," she replied, smiling at the thought. "Right, first thing is to have you fit and healthy once more, there's your baby to consider."

"No, no, not me, there must be some mistake!" still not wanting to believe the reality I had been denying for so long.

"I'm sorry Marie, but you must know it's the truth, my midwife friend estimates it's already eight to ten weeks into your pregnancy."

Left alone to mull over the future, I was soon overwhelmed by a whirlwind of emotions, dissolving into floods of tears; the sobbing lasting many hours, until exhaustion had me fall into a troubled slumber.

Coming to terms with this took many weeks, during

which Celeste ignored my tantrums, encouraging some regular exercise and conjuring up delicious meals for me. Her skilled bartering at the local market had vegetables exchanged for cheese or fish, maybe a chicken if no prying eyes were around.

So, slowly but surely, this surly waif changed to a more rounded young lady, still slim, but now signs of what was to come were showing.

"This is excellent my dear," she exclaimed, circling round me. "You're next check-up is due soon, so we must keep up the good work. Have you had any thoughts to the future, given that this damned war continues?"

"Having been part of the madness afflicting this world and knowing nothing else, what is there left?" I queried wearily.

"All things are possible, if one tries."

"Maybe, but what about falling in love during that crazy time," I wailed, blurting it all out. "It seems so stupid and utterly senseless now."

"No, never say that, true love comes but once and is impossible to resist, regardless of the time or place," stated Celeste quietly. "Don't blame yourself, everyone's lives are littered with such agonies, it's called being human."

"But I can't even mourn my losses after what a desire for revenge wrought," came with a sob.

"We all have a cross to bear, my dear."

I often wondered about my new friend's all day excursions to the local town, so one evening the question was broached.

"Well, as you know, I have to barter our garden produce for a variety of different foods which we enjoy," stated Celeste. "Plus, there are other clientele to satisfy."

"What customers are they?" was my obvious question.

"The ones willing to pay for sexual gratification," she explained. "Don't look so shocked my dear, in this present predicament, we all have to make sacrifices to survive; thank God I'm good at pleasuring men!"

"But, there are other ways, surely?"

"Not if you are in France illegally. You see, just before the war began, my then lover persuaded me to leave Italy and accompany him to Lyon. Unfortunately, many months later, when the invasion of France began, he panicked, running off to Marseille and pastures new; leaving me to fend for myself. To cut a long story short, I sold all his possessions, then begged, borrowed and stole enough to come here and settle down."

"My, you are one determined lady," full of admiration, until a thought struck me. "Does your clientele include Vichy supporters?"

"Of course," she interrupted quickly," but also members of the Resistance, who are appreciative of the information I can extract from their enemy. Don't worry, I'm no friend of any Fascist type, but business is business. Let's hope the future brings freedom for everyone."

CHAPTER TWELVE
'Birth, Loss And Blackmail'
Languedoc, France, 1944

Convinced by her explanations, we continued to live happily together as my pregnancy advanced; then rumours of a successful Allied invasion on the Normandy beaches reached us. This joyous news was tempered by apprehension, fears of a 'scorched earth' policy like that on the Eastern Front were very real. However, we were left alone by the Nazis, though two months later, confirmation of a successful American led invasion in the south of France; had the Wehrmacht, along with the Vichy officials and Militia men, virtually disappear overnight.

The Maquis resistance fighters liberated our area first, a cause of much celebration, excitement and relief, though all too soon they moved on northwards; leaving a somewhat dazed population to welcome the Allied troops.

Freedom had come at a colossal price, leaving the country and its economy in ruins, yet the population's first act was to initiate a tide of retribution against all those considered Nazi collaborators, or traitors. Much was made of the arrests and trials of high profile Vichy officials, but elsewhere, the countryside was being scoured for Militia men and informers. Scores of men and women were rounded up and tried in public, their sentences normally carried out immediately. That some of these people were innocent cannot be denied, but, baying mobs and firing squads don't discriminate!

 In the middle of all this and heavy with child, I thought my waters had broken; having Celeste escort me to my bed, then rush off to find her midwife friend. The next weeks were an agony of expectation, but nothing happened; even if I could feel the child kicking inside me. The actual birth was a torrid time, with me bathed in sweat, writhing around while others exhorted me to 'push'; dear God, as if I wasn't already trying my best!
 "Just one more," they falsely claimed; until at last, the pain died away and I heard a cry. "It's a boy!" Overheated and panting from exertion, when presented with the tiny form wrapped in a white towel, something unforgiveable happened, I fainted!

 Not two weeks later, when I and baby Andre were in the garden enjoying the afternoon sun; a serious looking Celeste joined us.
 "Right my girl, we can't delay this decision any longer," she began. "Whether you like it or not, Marie, you cannot give the child an upbringing it deserves. Being the young mother of an illegitimate child who has no home, money or other means of support, it simply isn't possible."
 "But, surely we can find a way."
 "No, the war will soon be over and I'm impatient to return to Italy," she reminded me. "Which means this property will be sold; then what will you do?"
 "I don't know, baby Andre has been my life of late."
 "For God's sake, Marie, please concentrate on the facts," Celeste said in a raised voice. "Remember, it was a desire for excitement and revenge that have you

in this situation; unfortunately, there's a price to pay for what that entailed. The only way to give this poor mite any kind of a future; is to have the nuns at Saint Cecilia's take him in."

"What can they do, that I can't?"

"Practically everything," she exclaimed, in an annoyed tone. "The nuns are perfectly capable of looking after very young children, while carefully vetting any couples who may wish to adopt your child. Rest assured, the lucky pair will give Andre a safe and happy childhood in a loving home."

So, that was that, despite all my screaming refusals, pleading or attempts at blackmail, Andre disappeared one night, never to be seen again. Awakening to find him gone had me hysterical, though Celeste refused to answer the insistent questioning; until I gave up and sank into a deep depression.

The following months must have been a trial for her, having to cope with this silent, morose individual who would burst into tears at the slightest excuse; but she never complained. Instead, I was guided to the garden, where long hours were spent harvesting and preparing the ground for new crops. Working there until colder days made it futile exercise, my pain and anger had lessened, meaning life returned to some semblance of normality; even if the following long winter nights sorely tested my resolve. However, for the rest of my life, it felt like a part of me was missing.

In the spring, when Paris was back in control of the country, our town settled back into its previous ways, even the local Mayor and Gendarmerie returned to assume their roles in society. I had thought that my previous life could be forgotten, leaving Celeste and I to continue our rural existence; which we did up to May the eighth, when the war finally ended. Dragged out to join the mad celebrations, several days passed before we recovered from it all, but, on returning to our sober and workaday selves, we were confronted by two men, who turned up on the doorstep.

"I wish to speak with Marie Angelique Montagne," one of them asked, having me acknowledge the fact. "Would it be possible for us to be on our own?"

Taking him to one side, our conversation had my fragile grip of normality almost fall apart, for these former Resistance figures were intent on persuading me to do their bidding. I was told about a small group of private bankers who had loaned the Vichy government money, traitors whose financial clout had now allowed them to resume their pre-war positions, most living openly in Lyon or Marseille. "Because of a known expertise in these matters, you have been selected to carry out their elimination," was said with an air of authority.

"Sorry, those days are over, the judicial system should deal with them," I shot back.

"I beg to differ," he replied. "These men cannot be allowed to escape due punishment; so, any refusal on your part, will result in Paris being told about the Ardennes incident in nineteen-forty-three."

Oh great, the past had come back to haunt me; so, left with no choice, I submitted to the demand, agreeing to do their dirty work. Before these two 'vigilantes' left, I was given some money, the necessary information and a full magazine of bullets for my Beretta.

I returned to the house, screaming at the injustice of it all; yes, the bloody war was over, but having lost absolutely everything because of it, my own people still wanted more of me. God, they were no better than the Nazis!

With my few possessions packed and ready for departure, I embraced the helpless Celeste, thanking her for every kindness, then left. Cycling away, my thoughts turned to where was there to run to, if and when everything went to plan; though no answers were forthcoming from my addled brain!

Things were difficult enough, for although gun crime was not unknown then, a group of rich people dying by the same method would surely ring alarm bells within the authorities. Therefore, a fatal 'car crash', unexpected 'heart attack' and one regrettable 'accident' at home, became the variety of my killings; all readily explainable, so no official investigations into the deaths were ever carried out. However, the remaining money man must have taken note of what happened and promptly disappeared. This gentleman was no fool, for it took months to track him down, only a lucky sighting had me informed he was presently in Menton, where I was dispatched to post haste.

This town, close to the borders of Italy and Monaco, seemed a curious place to be. With Italy equally destitute as France and Monaco the only haven for the wealthy, what was he waiting for; or did the authorities in Monte Carlo know something I didn't? Having no knowledge of this gentlemen bar what I had been told, it made me circumspect when shadowing his movements.

Monsieur Z, as he was named, was a cautious fellow, alternating the routes to favoured shops and cafés; the sly, but detailed observations of his surroundings telling me this was a person who was well used to taking precautions. So, it meant the only place where he could relax, was inside his present accommodation; which no doubt was fortified in some way.

Problem was, said accommodation happened to be a second floor apartment, complete with a full length balcony; the only way in for me, for the presence of a concierge meant walking into this building without a reason, was impossible. Happily, some luxuriant plant growth outside meant, if it could support my weight, reaching the balcony was possible.

When the time came, darkness and a hidden drainpipe, plus some added support from the greenery, had me up to and in front of the apartment's glazed doors in no time. Now, breaking into a property isn't one of my talents, but surprisingly, one of the doors was found to be unlocked. Not believing this happened to be mere carelessness, I silently moved inside with my Beretta at the ready, only to find there was nobody in any of the rooms. Odd, because I saw Monsieur Z enter the apartment building alone, not ten minutes back. There was no time to think about this, for there the sound of a key entering the front door lock signalled its opening, allowing a well-dressed woman and my target to come inside.

Oh damn, this was an unexpected problem, there had been so sign of any romantic liaison previously. But it wasn't, for a sheath of documents appeared from her bag as two brandies were delivered; followed by a business like discussion, which ended with both of them signing a page, then a toast. Brandies drunk, the woman shook hands with my target and left. Oh Lord,

I thought, was this the prelude to entering Monaco unhindered? If so, the elimination must happen now.

Closing the front door, Monsieur Z returned to stare out of the balcony windows.

"Okay, you can come out now, I've been expecting a visit for some time," he said loudly, turning to see me stood in front of him, a pistol aimed at his head. "Well, well, this is novel, a female assassin, do you mind if the condemned man has a final cigarette?"

Before I could say no, he dived swiftly to the left as his right hand reached inside the jacket, so my first shot only winged him. Recovering in a flash, his automatic pistol replied; the bullet tearing into my left side, the agonising pain having me falter, allowing him to aim again. But, pulling the trigger did nothing, for his gun had jammed! A split second later the puzzled looking man died, as my second shot had a bullet enter his heart.

"Note for your next life, Monsieur Z: when buying an automatic pistol, insist on a Beretta, an Italian made weapon with a reputation for reliability!" came as I slipped out of the same glazed door used when entering. Question for self, why did I close the damn thing after slipping inside the apartment?

In my haste to reach solid ground, I lost grip of the drainpipe and fell, stifling a scream of agony upon landing. Hobbling away as fast as possible, the sound of whistles and pounding footsteps soon reaching me; was this quick reaction due to the mystery female?

Having been blackmailed by my former comrades in the Resistance to commit murder and now a wanted person in France and Monaco, my future was looking bleak; but, this was no time to deliberate, I had to act fast.

CHAPTER THIRTEEN
'Naples, Pain And Despair'
Italy, 1946

Decision made; one skinny female and rucksack ventured forth to find, where despite the presence of Allied troops, or perhaps because of them, the border crossing into Italy presented few challenges. However, travel further south was problematic, the roads were in atrocious condition and non-military transport virtually invisible, so the only alternative was to go by train. Papa had always warned me off the railway, for once on board, you are trapped inside carriages with no means of escape; but, in this case, speed was of the essence.

 If I was expecting a passenger train there was disappointment, the only rail traffic was goods trains, mostly full of military equipment. Did I mention speed, well the journey to Genoa inside an empty wagon was the opposite, the slow moving train stopping many times for unspecified reasons; annoying, but it gave me time to consider things. Deciding to stay far away from Menton for the foreseeable future; for some unknown reason, the historic city of Naples was my choice, even though I had never been there, nor experienced urban life. With that in mind, Genoa to Rome was the next train ride, which happily was a faster one than before, but throughout it my gunshot wound started aching abominably. With all my organs presumably functioning correctly, I guessed the bullet had missed everything important, while gentle probing convinced me that there was nothing left inside the wound. However, the area didn't look too good and with no access to medical help, it remained a worry.

Feeling worse on arrival in Rome, things were further complicated by having to find the goods yard from which south bound trains left. The long hikes had me exhausted, so the last of my money was spent on a few morsels of food. Trudging through the streets, I met others struggling to reach the same destination, so we joined forces in the search for the ideal transport.

If you call wagonload after wagonload of damaged tanks and other military equipment ideal, then this was it, for there were several cattle trucks tacked on the end of it. Creeping on board one in the dead of night, we then waited a further twenty-four hours before a locomotive was coupled up and we moved off, slowly. Asking how long the trip might take, I was told normally around twelve hours, although that would now be a minor miracle according to my fellow 'passengers'.

I remember little of that journey, for the pain from my wound steadily increased in intensity, while a fever developed. Exhaustion soon overtook me, but the fitful slumbers contained lurid coloured nightmares of my past, leading to periods of sweaty and confused wakefulness. As time passed, the pain became so unbearable I thought the end was in sight; oh well, what the hell, my life had turned into a total nightmare, was it really worth fighting the inevitable?

CHAPTER FOURTEEN
'Salvation, A Friend And more'
Naples, Italy, 1945

I awoke between crisp, white sheets again, but this time there was no scented aroma, nor friendly face to greet me. This bare, antiseptic looking room smelt strongly of disinfectant and a grim faced nun stood alongside my iron bedstead.

"Good morning, young lady," came from an elderly gentleman, dressed in a white coat; but why was he addressing me in atrocious English? No matter, after telling him I understood a little Italian, he then launched into rapid fire explanations of my arrival here. It seemed a worker at the rail yard had found my comatose body, contacted this Catholic charity hospital, whose staff brought me here.

No question was ever asked of how I acquired my injury; only that the bullet wound was badly infected, having them worried gangrene might take hold. An operation had been performed, removing the infected tissue, while some of their meagre supply of penicillin had been administered to prevent further problems. This now appeared to be successful, but the resulting scars were for life. After digesting that information, I thanked them wholeheartedly and promised to repay their kindness in any way possible, upon reaching full fitness.

When that day came, I was set to work, toiling long

and hard, sweeping, then mopping all the corridors and wards of the building. Moving on to wash and iron a never ending flow of soiled bedding; finishing off by repainting the used and abused doors and window frames, where needed! All this being carried out under the watchful eye of a senior nun, whose standards were, of necessity, very high. How long I stayed there is anyone's guess, but the seasons changed, with me glad to be insulated from the cold. When warmer weather returned, I considered the debt to them repaid, leaving the hospital with my senior nun's blessing. Having no idea when or where the Beretta disappeared, I ventured forth, equipped with only my few clothes, knife and rucksack.

It was not a happy time, all too soon the deafening cacophony of this city, plus the non-stop hustle and bustle of its people wore me down; an urban life wasn't for me. So, where to go, venturing south meant passing the recently active Vesuvius, something which had me uncharacteristically nervous. So north it was, trudging along hugging the coast, passing through rundown fishing villages and farming communities; dear Lord, was there no end to the post war privations? Depressed by the sight of this never ending poverty; when happening upon a small uninhabited cove, I slumped down on its sandy beach and stared blankly out to sea.

"Hey you! Yes you, there's no one else around is there?" interrupted my black thoughts. I looked up to see a short, scrawny young man, beckoning me over. Dressed in a worn, collarless shirt and shorts, his long brown hair framed a tanned countenance, which lit up when he smiled.

"You look in need of a decent meal, fancy some fish?" had me nodding, only for him to remove his threadbare clothing and stride for the sea in his underpants.

"How are you going to catch them?" I called, on noting there was no sign of a rod or net.

"With my hands, stupid," was the disparaging reply.

Intrigued, I watched as he dived continuously until satisfied with his catch. However, there was no sign of any fish when he returned. Imagine my surprise when they were proudly extracted from inside his underpants!

"I have no money for a net," he explained earnestly, removing a penknife from his shorts and gutting the catch; this treasured possession was then carefully cleaned and used to cut wood for a fire. Small shavings were ignited by some device on the knife, giving us a roaring fire in no time. A few minutes later I wolfed down my first meal for days; finished off with cool water from a military water bottle he extracted from the wet sand.

"Feeling better?" my benefactor enquired. "By the way, my name is Emilio, aspiring artist and designer; and you?"

"Marie, originally from Belgium, with no particular aspirations, the war..." I faltered, unwilling to continue.

"Is best forgotten," Emilio continued for me. "Everyone must now concentrate on the future," which meant there was never any talk of his life and times, let alone possible family.

One thing was certain though; he was artistically brilliant, the creations he formed in the sand were truly beautiful and inspiring. He also appeared ambitious and hungry for success, but was disheartened by knowing the best places to display his talents were cities in the industrial north, Milan and Turin.

They seemed an impossible distance away and anyway, I was content just to enjoy the sun, sea and sand, swimming or making love on our private beach; a totally new experience for me. As long as the balmy weather continued I was happy to stay there, only occasionally did the two of us have to venture inland to barter fish for some fruit or vegetables.

But, as with everything, I eventually tired of this simple life, suggesting we should do something about Emilio's ambitions. But, he was enthusiastic one minute and dithery the next; seemingly unable to make a decision, which had our conversation turn to other things. Weeks later and near the end of my tether, I demanded we move on and head north, even if we had to walk all the way. To my surprise he concurred, but cautioned that with no money, two knives and little else, we would struggle to overcome the obvious difficulties.

"Nothing ventured, nothing gained; let's do it," I cried, somehow overly eager to move on.

After trudging along many kilometres of empty, minor roads, it was a disappointment to see the main highway to Rome also sparsely trafficked. These two ragged travellers found obtaining a lift was virtually impossible, until some soldiers in an American military vehicle took pity on us; even having us share their rations as we headed north. Luckily, Emilio could speak some English, so we learnt what had been happening in the world; plus local conditions in the Eternal city, before being dropped off at its outskirts.

As we made our way to the city centre, where just like Naples, yet more bomb damaged buildings greeted us; with no sign of any rebuilding. It was patently obvious most of the population were unemployed and near starvation, desperate times for the gangs of men hanging around at street corners, who viewed us two with suspicion. The chances of making some money here were already looking doomed to fail.

"Don't get downhearted, Marie, regardless of what happens in this world, the rich always stay that way," Emilio assured me. "We just have to find them."

Well, knowing where the wealthier suburbs were situated, find them he did! After a series of rejections, one gentleman gave Emilio a trial, to undo a little of the years of neglect in the family's palatial residence, restoring its painted ceilings and murals. As this required knowledge and experience, which my friend clearly had, he was eventually properly employed and received a substantial wage.

With nothing to do, Emilio suggested I find a native speaker to teach me English, something he considered would be important in the coming years. Complying with his wish led to more than expected, for I discovered a penchant for the language, reaching fluency in record time, much to my tutor's delight. This lady also found a job for me, modelling clothes at an up market shop; which had me introduced to people from all over Western Europe, especially Paris.

Well, well, Mother's hard schooling was finally paying off, for being petite, but with a good figure; while knowing how to look my best, behave and converse with the best of society, it soon brought offers of advancement. The only down side was the scarring left by my bullet wound; yes, they had begun to fade, but I knew it meant modelling some garments was impossible, because leading couturiers in France required unblemished skin. Then there was the thorny question of my identity papers, I had none!

However, although prospective employers knew all this, an offer came I couldn't refuse; along with the promise of a new passport and I.D. card! So, after a tearful farewell to Emilio, this now French citizen accompanied by my employer's agent flew; yes, my first scary ride in an aeroplane, all the way to Paris! Walking out of Orly airport, I looked around, impatient to start living in this unknown and very different world.

CHAPTER FIFTEEN
'A New Life, Love And Death'
Paris, France, 1948

After staying the night in a cheap hotel, the agent collected me and we went by taxi to an old warehouse, located at the city outskirts; where the inside was divided into various storage and dressmaking sections, both very busy. Handed over to a stern looking woman in a small, cold room, she had me stripped down to my underclothes, only to be given a pair of high heeled shoes to wear; standing around shivering, while waiting for the 'top man' to arrive.

 When this gentleman deemed to show his face, it was a theatrical entrance, a cape and hat being removed with a flourish, revealing a painfully thin figure, dressed in an immaculate blue suit and shoes to match. There was a single, black glove on his right hand, contrasting nicely with the shock of white hair, piercing dark eyes and expressive mouth. He marched up to me, leisurely walking around, viewing me from every angle, then stopped, deliberating some more; until his gloved hand was thrust into the air, which had a female assistant come running.

"This one is small, but perfectly formed, so she will henceforth be known as 'Miss Angel'", he declared. "Come my dear, there is much work to be done." Hurriedly dressing, I was rushed outside, joining him inside a large, pre-war car, painted cream and black;

which sped off into the city. Arriving at the back of some commercial building, we alighted, entering an area of heavenly aromas and eager ladies; beauticians and hairdressers, who began work at my escort's word. Primped, powdered, perfumed and ready, I was ushered to his presence once again, where he stood looking at racks of dresses. There were many um's and ah's before he selected one for me to wear; an assistant magically appearing to help me change, then both set about adjusting the fit. Without knowing why, during this performance I couldn't help but point at my scars; which had the chief designer look at me. Removing his glove, it revealed a livid red and brown mangled hand with two missing fingers.

"Forget little imperfections, my dear," he breathed quietly, slipping its black covering back on. "Right, your presence has recharged my creative drive, some ideas have come to mind. Until they become reality, get changed and familiarise yourself with your new surroundings; then prepare yourself to be very busy." As it turned out, that was an understatement!

I was found somewhere to live, a tiny apartment in a large, overcrowded block; which wasn't appreciated. But, as most evenings were taken up with showing off the latest fashions in fancy restaurants, theatres or private events; it served only as a bed and breakfast unit, which suited me just fine.

During the quiet moments of these forays, I questioned Alain, the chief designer, about our fashion house. He was very candid, revealing the business was run on a shoestring; everything I had seen was leased or borrowed. However, theatrical behaviour combined with glitz and glamour, were considered necessary to project success to their well-off customers; even if that ate into any profit. What he really needed to do was come up with wildly popular designs, ones that could be worn by women of all shapes and sizes, plus be manufactured cheaply, by them and any licensees. With that mass market appeal, sales would boom; hopefully leading to worldwide recognition for the company, allowing him to concentrate on true haute couture. Unfortunately, he rightly observed, this would only be achieved by inspiration, hard work and a large slice of luck.

 So, plunged into this precarious world of dreams, I soon learnt that stamina was a required quality, for the hours were long, the constant travel exhausting, while pandering to fussy photographers was extremely irritating. All this and having to look one's absolute best at all times, it was enough to make you scream; especially those days where nothing went according to plan. Mind you, the perks included free, luxury travel and hotels, plus a chance to appreciate cordon blue cooking and taste the finest wines, all in moderation, of course! Curiously, although I quickly discovered most fashion models were a lot younger, nobody, but nobody ever asked my age; this insecurity had me gaze into a mirror on occasion, wondering why not. Nevertheless, my new life was more exciting than lethally dangerous, like before. Plus, I had somewhere to live and was paid; more than enough positives to keep me at it!
I mustn't forget the steady stream of ardent suitors. These could be a pleasant distraction or an absolute nightmare, depending on the situation; but sadly, none gave me the thrills I experienced with Andre. Their attention and caresses were gratefully accepted, while the love making was fulfilling, but a vital

emotion was lacking; so much so, I despaired of meeting another true love. Not that these young men stopped coming, whenever they knew 'Miss Angel' would be around!

From then on, fully established in the small team of models and popular with the clients, my busy life had time pass in a dizzying blur, the austere post-war period fading into memory as the fashion house grew and prospered. Some of Alain's designs had proved good money spinners, but none were the real success story he craved. He laboured on convinced the time would come; while looking over his shoulder at the increasing competition.

Meanwhile, the Cold War cast a long shadow over a continent now intent on peace, while the ever changing governments in Paris had things go from bad to worse in faraway Indochina and Algeria; let alone fomenting unrest closer to home. Despite this and gloomy economic forecasts, life improved for the majority, having most set out to enjoy long overdue good times. On a personal note, because the Second World War, occupation and its aftermath, still loomed large in the nation's conscience, one niggling question haunted my waking hours; would my past return again and shatter the dream? To my relief, so far no stranger had ever come knocking at my door, to deliver bad news.

In nineteen-fifty-four something remarkable happened, Alain struck gold, his design for a simple, black cocktail dress became an instant hit. As he and our team dashed all over the country to show it off, sales rocketed, attracting attention from elsewhere.

Europe fell under its spell and within months, ladies all over the world were clamouring to have a genuine Alain Karsch creation in their wardrobe. Profits mushroomed overnight, sending the company to number one position in fashion; a situation which had investors and manufacturers knocking on our door, all eager for a share of this good fortune.
"All well and good," commented our chief designer. "But you are only as good as the last success, so back to the drawing board!" Then, contrary as ever, he ignored his own advice, having everyone's wages increased; my already substantial salary increasing accordingly.

This windfall finally decided me to invest in a property, having all spare time dedicated to scanning realtor's offerings. Eventually, I settled on a single storey villa near Biarritz, which nestled inside the pine woods; but whose garden had views out over the ocean. After having negotiated a good price, it was mine; then the hard work began. Little did I realise an eagle eye was required to keep contractors on track, when working on the alterations required to make it my home. With my itinerary of constant travel, it made having a car imperative, so a Citroen DS was purchased, this beautiful, blue machine being used and abused on untold high speed journeys across Western Europe.

Ever since joining the fashion house, I had enjoyed a special relationship with Alain; for both of us instinctively knew that there were secrets in our lives that could never be revealed. Apart from the fact he was born in Eastern Europe, but surfaced in Paris during in the mid-thirties, claiming to be a fashion designer of note; I knew nothing of his life. There were rumours of course, claims of his homosexuality, double dealing and collaboration with the Nazis were quoted; but the truth was probably stranger than fiction! Despite the necessary flamboyance when working, he remained a very private person, who steadfastly refused my suggestion for plastic surgery on the damaged hand.

"Never, my dear," he insisted. "It serves as a reminder of past mistakes and what might have been," leaving me to guess what that meant.

I suppose it was this friendship and his endearing enthusiasm that kept me going, for after over a decade in the business, how many times had I toyed with the idea of ending this exhausting career? When my new home was finished, that idea came to the fore; just entering the front door gave me a warm, fuzzy feeling, happy to be inside my little slice of heaven.

Hardly had my decision been made, when a new man walked into my life, having me head over heels in love again. My new beau was Marc Defarge, a tall, dark and handsome man; with a smile that melted my heart. A war hero turned millionaire businessman, who had the ear of those with power, be they politicians or fellow entrepreneurs; meant this man did nothing by halves. The whirlwind romance had us in a bewildering array of five star hotels, swanky restaurants and society get-togethers, mingling with the glitterati as he exchanged information and made deals. Then it was off to some nightclub, creeping back to our bed for some intense love making.

His main leisure pursuit was horse racing, having us attend all the premiere meetings, where outrageous friends and hangers-on gathered to drink large quantities of fine wine and wager vast sums on the runners; all for thrill of the chase! Most ended the day intoxicated and a lot poorer.

Having decided not to renew my contract for nineteen-sixty, everyone at the fashion house thought Marc and I were going to be married, probably in Nice. Come departure time, it was a beautiful summer's day; where tearful farewells from all my friends had me almost regretting my decision to leave. But leave I did, being driven off south to live the dream. Like most of what he did, this journey was done at breakneck speed in his Facel Vega coupe; Marc's casual driving style having me cowering in the passenger seat. I swear we only slowed down once, then only to show off when cruising along the seafront road of our destination!
No sooner were we installed in his impressive cliff top mansion, than the champagne lifestyle started once more; luxury yachts moored in the harbour became the scene of riotous parties and impromptu bathing. While more of the same continued on land, for the bars and nightclubs were full of the 'beautiful people' having a good time.
Wonderful as all this was, the nonstop revelry was wearing me down, exhaustion bringing on blinding headaches, which no ordinary remedies could relieve. Complaining of this to Marc, had him laugh at first, then say there was a cure all for my problems in his private office. When a bag of white powder appeared, the realisation his full on, non-stop lifestyle was fuelled by drugs had me in shock. Furthermore, going by the amount of cocaine being snorted, the drug was taking over his life. Now, admittedly, witnessing this

was nothing new for me, the high pressure atmosphere in Paris had created widespread drug abuse, but when it concerns the one you love, it rendered me speechless.

Recovering my voice, I begged him to consider the damage he was doing to himself and stop, promising to find help if he did. My pleas were brushed aside; he could handle it, a blatant lie and one which led to bad feelings between us. Increasing moodiness and periods of hyper activity told me he was still at it; then things came to a head one sultry, August evening. I was in the bedroom nursing a migraine as he prepared to go out; when learning I had no intention of accompanying him, my normally attentive lover turning into an absolute monster. After a nonsensical shouting match, he stormed off out, rear wheels spitting gravel as the Facel Vega roared away. I retired to my darkened room, falling asleep after the prescribed pills took effect.

I was awoken by the police at three o'clock in the morning, a worried looking female officer reporting that Marc and a female passenger had died in a traffic accident, on the road to Monaco. My grief was tempered by the fact, that it had taken him little time to find another female companion.

Next day, the newspaper headlines were all about this tragedy, mourning the death of France's 'star' couple. I did nothing to refute this mistake, having already fled before dawn, heading for my private hideaway near Biarritz; wanting no more than to be left alone. The disillusion, grief and despair brought back the pain of losing baby Andre, having me descend into a suicidal depression; days passing in an alcoholic haze before I finally came to my senses.

Alone, but coherent again, it was now time for some gentle pottering about.

Only one visitor came knocking, though thankfully it was a taxi which brought Alain to my door, not his vast, over the top, pre-war vehicle. There were no theatrics this time; his smart casual clothing suited my location, and the sincere condolences were accepted.

The weather was sublime during his short stay, having us outside most of the time; though the simple, al fresco meals I prepared were lost on him. Perhaps my perfunctory waitress style was not to his liking! One morning, after spending time examining the garden's colourful flowers and shrubs, he stopped and turned to look at me.

"Methinks serious thought should be given to what you will do from now on," he intoned gently. "Forget the previous disaster; sadly, it wouldn't have lasted anyway. Direct your energies to something fulfilling, but make it a lifelong endeavour."

"I have already made arrangements for that," I informed him, telling him of my intentions. "Your input would be most helpful, at least to start with."

"I am willing to share some snippets of insider knowledge for a while, but after that you are on your own."

"Thank you Alain; now what about you, does the world of fashion design still have you in its thrall?" I enquired.

"Oh yes, unlike you, I am a city boy whose ambitions will always remain the same; to continually beat my competitors at their own game. I will probably die still clutching a sketch pad in my hand!"

"Hopefully that won't be for some time yet," I concluded, as we stood gazing out to sea, whilst enjoying the sun's comforting warmth.

Questioned by reporters about my disappearance before he came to see me, they were told only that I had left the company's employ to start a new life; which, as they already knew had ended in tragedy. Hopefully that was an end to it all, but as always, there was that niggling doubt at the back of my mind.

CHAPTER SIXTEEN
'Blackmail Again'
Biarritz, France, 1960

After Alain returned to Paris, you wouldn't have recognised me, sans make up and the fancy clothes, I pottered around the place with my hair tied back, wearing an old, worn pair of overalls; preparing the house for winter. Mind you, the odd sunny day had me relaxing amidst the fading glory of summer flowers, lying back on a beach towel, occasionally drifting off into pleasant dreams. It was one such day like this, when I received a rude awakening.

"Ahem, Madame! Wake up, Madame!" came an insistent voice, as I blinked, looking up to see two men in black suits standing in front of me.

"What the hell are you doing in my garden?" was my indignant response, incensed by this intrusion. "This is private property. Leave now, or I will call the police."

"I'm afraid our authority far exceeds your local Gendarmerie's remit," the better dressed figure stated, moving forward to help me up. "Shall we sit at the table over there; I have been instructed to tell you of an important role you can play for your country, regarding a matter of increasing urgency."

This sparked my curiosity, so we moved over and sat down; this nondescript, average looking individual facing me, while his companion stayed where he was.

"You have a nice place here, Marie; or should I call you, 'Miss Angel'?"

"I beg your pardon, my name is Mlle Bergamont to strangers; you are?"

"Let us say, my friend and I are representatives of a higher authority," was the smooth reply.

"And who might they be?"

"Will mentioning the Surete, Interior Ministry, or the Elysee Palace suffice?" he replied, passing an official document to me. Reading it, an ice cold chill shot down my spine, this cosy little existence of mine was about to be blown apart.

"So, what is it they want?" I asked with a heavy heart.

"You may have read newspaper reports about recent threats and unrest stirred up by a secret organisation devoted to overturning any decision concerning the future of an independent Algeria. Well, before events get out of hand, those on high have decided that their chief 'agent provocateur' should be dealt with; you are their chosen instrument."

"Why me, don't the security services have a specialist unit for this sort of thing?" any excuse to avoid what was coming next.

"I'm unaware of any such organisation," he replied. "But, as no government involvement could be countenanced at this sensitive juncture, a solo operation was considered correct."

"So, how am I supposed to do this terrible deed?" was my complaint. "Being a fashion model didn't transform me into some murderer for hire, you know."

"Oh, come, come, Marie, you were well trained by your late father, one of, if not the best contract killers in Belgium during pre-war days," he stated knowingly. "Plus, later Resistance activities showed there was a certain flair for this kind of work."

"That was a long time ago, the occupation forced many people, including me, to do regrettable things."

"Maybe, but some of these 'things' were done after it ended," he emphasised.

"Meaning, any refusal on my part, would have every detail of them become public knowledge?"

"Quite so," he intimated, casting his eyes around my property. "It would be a shame to lose all this by saying one little word. Life could become very difficult for you," a threat intended to have me submit, no doubt.

"As you probably know, there are no weapons kept here, so am I expected to pay for all that this assassination requires?" fully expecting it to be true.

"A suitable firearm will be delivered to your door, though not by the usual channels," I was assured. "On completion of the task, arrangements will be made for its disposal." With that, a photograph and two pages of information about my target were passed over; after which he wished me good day and turned to leave, joining his companion, they walked off to disappear via the beach.

Absolutely furious, but knowingly helpless, I rushed indoors to scream and shout at the uncomprehending walls; fully aware my adopted country had lined me up for blackmail, years ago!

CHAPTER SEVENTEEN
'Cote D'Azur, The First Contract'
Biarritz, France, 1959

Shaking off my despondency, I set about my allotted task; as Papa always said, preparation was ninety per cent of it. Firstly, what did the papers tell me?

The black and white photograph showed a tall, athletic-looking man with tanned skin, thinning dark hair, grey eyes and a facial scar that turned his smile to more of a sneer.

The target's name was Pierre Auguste, thirty eight years old, a retired Army officer, whose family owned one of the largest trading companies in Oran, Algeria. Being a brilliant tactician and organiser he was once considered the military's rising star, having served with distinction in Indochina and North Africa.

On foundation of the Fifth Republic, it had him posted back to France, where he repeatedly clashed with senior officers over future plans for Algerian independence and was asked to resign. He did so and left for home, though within a year he returned to Marseille, where all contact was lost. A later police raid had him caught speaking at a meeting of Pied Noir sympathisers in Paris; whose connections to other anti-government groups subsequently grew stronger, their threats and demonstrations becoming more targeted. He had no known address in this country, but was a frequent guest of influential friends, who live on the Cote d'Azur. Their addresses were written below.

Well, well, so basically, he is a rich kid who will do anything to protect his inheritance! In that case I should follow the money, heading south east to a playground of the wealthy. Then, if my target makes an appearance, the countdown can begin.
A few days later, a garden machinery company van delivered one weighty, but not overly large package to my door. Having signed the receipt and heaved it indoors, the supposed heavy duty hedge trimmer revealed itself as an aluminium case. The inside was lined with foam rubber, where a lightweight, but curiously designed, automatic pistol, plus all the components to convert to a rifle, lay protected. Fully assembled, its matt black finish belied the obvious quality of construction, though predictably, there was no makers mark or serial number to be found. However, a loaded magazine, telescopic sight, silencer, tool kit and oil bottle were supplied. Having seen but one example of this type before, albeit dating from the early nineteen-hundreds, I had no doubts as to where it was manufactured; in Germany.
A short trip out into the woods followed, but a mere three rounds was all it took to have this rifle's sights adjusted to my needs. Hmm, a well-made, quickly assembled, extremely accurate and powerful weapon; it's almost as if the designer could have been a sniper, perhaps he or she was!

Crossing the country in my beloved, but easily recognisable DS was a non-starter, as was my fanciful idea of swopping it for an all-black version. The irony of driving a favourite of the French authorities had an appeal, though those on high definitely wouldn't be amused. After a period of head scratching, I decided to leave the DS on my drive, just visible to passersby; while a trip to Lyon had a pastel coloured Peugeot 403 hired for a couple of weeks.

The cross country jaunts were completed in speedy comfort, even if the last part of my journey saw me splashing through heavy rain along the south east coast road. On the approach to Nice, all that water made a call of nature become ever more urgent; so pulling over into the next available petrol station, I stopped and ran for the toilets. Greatly relieved and refreshed after a quick wash, walking outside nearly had me run down by a Mercedes saloon, as it swerved round to stop alongside the petrol pumps. My indignation turned to surprise on noting the number plate; Holy Christ, it was my target's car! A quick backtrack to the Peugeot, had a hat rammed on my head and the gun in my coat pocket.

"Hey you, fill her up and check the oil," came a command, my slight hesitation rewarded by," and make it snappy, I have to be in Paris by morning."

Well, it's now or never, this chance encounter with Monsieur Auguste might be my last; thought she while doing as requested, checking the oil dipstick level as petrol continued to fill the tank.

"That will be fifty-four francs please, sir," I asked politely. "But there's no charge for this," came as the silencer pressed into his chest, the shot being inaudible due to a continuing downpour. Taking his wallet, the bill was hurriedly paid to a bored cashier, who grunted something when handing over the receipt; his eyes never leaving the nearby television screen. Perhaps he was disappointed the customer was no glamorous young lady, just another old woman bundled up against the cold and wet, the face virtually invisible.

Though hidden from the cashier's view, thankfully there were no other cars around either, so my target was heaved onto the passenger seat, allowing me to drive the Mercedes away. It took some time to find an out of the way parking place that was near a bus stop; unfortunately, the one I eventually chose was in a dark, rundown area, where shadowy figures flitted between the buildings. Waiting around had me somewhat unnerved by this, but the welcome sight of a bus approaching my stop, caused a sigh of relief. Arriving back at the petrol station, my Peugeot was quietly driven off and we headed back to Lyon, the hypnotic flick of its windscreen wipers continuing as the rain continued non-stop.

As my previous visits had been brief and work oriented, with little time for leisure, I stayed and explored the city until the car was due to be returned; though there were no newspaper headlines about a shooting in Nice. Had my 'handlers' been watching all along and quickly removed the evidence? This was something to mull over as my elaborate journey home continued. On arrival, all seemed to be well, my blue DS was still on the driveway, dusty but untouched; while inside the house, it also appeared unsullied. But, there was one tell-tale sign of interference, the small scrap of paper I had jammed between my bedroom door and its frame, now lay on the floor. Oh, just what had my blackmailers been up to now?

Refraining from making more noise than necessary, I crept around examining all the lights, telephone, electrical appliances and other convenient nooks and crannies; but no additional items being found on any of them. Also, there was no sign of interference, or new wiring, in the fuse box; hmm, all very curious. Going outside, the garden seemed the same, though, as expected, the grass had grown. Even checking all around the roof for a hidden aerial or wiring, it revealed nothing out of the ordinary. Okay, were you clever buggers just playing mind games; or was there really some device embedded in my house or garage?

Deciding there must be; every cubby hole, wardrobe and cupboard was emptied, thoroughly checked, then put back together; the furniture was moved around, while carpets, rugs, along with all wall hangings and curtains were removed and cleaned. It was probably the best winter spruce up this house had ever had! But alas, there was no sign of any small electrical device; which left but one other option, the car.

Grovelling underneath it had me trying to remember Papa's teachings, so to my untutored eye everything was as it should be; with no added extras! However, the handbook wasn't much use for making any sense of the mass of pipes and wires that lay beneath the bonnet, making a trip to the garage imperative.

Bathed, perfumed and 'dressed to kill', I arrived there begging for the mechanics to check over my beautiful, blue machine. My designer clothes, teetering high heels and professional make up still worked, for the younger ones were soon falling over each other to impress; none more so than the lad who found a small, black box attached to what he called the 'C' pillar. He was rewarded with twenty francs and a kiss, though my simpering, dumb blonde act had changed to furious woman mode.

"A certain gentleman is going to regret this intrusion into my life," I told him, before paying the bill and leaving in a hurry.

Back at home, I examined the plain plastic box,

discerning it contained something magnetic, for it would attach itself to any metallic object; but for what purpose? My educated guess; could it be a radio transmitter, telling some receiver whereabouts the car was located. Further reading at the local library, told me the small size meant its range was limited; so, they, whoever they were, would have to follow wherever the car led them. Fanciful ideas about leading them round in circles for a day were dismissed; because this object could be a red herring, something easily found, thereby allaying my fears of being constantly monitored?

Okay, I had found nothing inside my house; that left the garden, which conveniently, was in need of cut back and clear up. So, courtesy of the damp weather it was back to overalls and wellingtons, every millimetre of the area from front gates to my private, beach access, being worked on.

Obsessive examination of every plant, bush and lawn revealed little, so the pine trees were then given special attention. Those in adjacent properties were left alone, but the ones on mine were viewed from behind, for logically, any device or camera, would have to face towards my house.

The results were alarming; two close to the beach had black boxes mounted between their trunks and a convenient branch! Close examination was impossible without giving the game away, while viewing them through binoculars from inside the house, told me little.

Damn it, I fumed, those swine were watching and following my every move; it was like being a rat in some weird laboratory experiment!

After calming down, another thought occurred to me; was all this done to make you assume that, for a paranoid person can be easily manipulated? Just look what that very thing was causing in the Cold War!

CHAPTER EIGHTEEN
'Paris Mayhem'
Biarritz, France, 1961

With Christmas and the New Year gone and forgotten, my thoughts turned to the weapon locked away in the attic; why had no communication arrived concerning its disposal? Was there another bogeyman the state wished to be rid of, by putting me in a dangerous situation once more? I had two months to mull over that, before the beach access saw my two 'handlers' turn up, wanting to talk.

"Good morning, Mlle Bergamont, I have news for you," said the smarter dressed one, having left his companion outside to keep watch. "Another problem has come to light, one which is deemed an immediate threat, therefore my masters have decreed this task must be expedited forthwith."

"Whoa there, before you start ordering me about," I replied firmly. "Firstly, an explanation regarding those two objects attached to my trees out there; secondly, they are then to be removed."

"Ah, those are the latest gems of battery powered, surveillance technology," he responded enthusiastically. "Unfortunately it's standard practice, to install them where there is a possibility of divided loyalties."

"Correct me if I'm wrong, but my first 'task' was carried out without complaint, was it not? As for your 'gems', no battery lasts the length of time those boxes have been there; nor has anyone been observed climbing the trees to change them."

"Maybe not, but don't underestimate progress, Marie," he concluded, handing over a photograph and just one page of notes. With that he left, joining his companion for a brief conversation; then they made for the beach access.

The photograph he left showed a medium height gentleman in casual clothes, whose muscular physique was emphasised by the studio pose. With severely short, black hair, hooded, but bright eyes and a swarthy, pock-marked complexion, his forced, tight-lipped smile was barely visible. Forty eight year old, Charles Firmin, obviously didn't like being in front of a camera! The notes had him as a former paratrooper and grizzled veteran of the Second World War, Indochina and his home country, Algeria, who rose through the ranks to become a Major. Retiring two years back, he was now known to be working for the OAS, by organising future funding and violent demonstrations. Based in Paris, he was rarely seen in public, but known to regularly change his accommodation.

Hmm, something told me, my 'handlers' had already interrogated someone close to my target; not helpful, as Monsieur Firmin would be aware of this arrest by now, confirming that the authorities were closing in on him.

While at Biarritz railway station checking on the times for Bordeaux, then Paris bound trains; I overheard a German talking to some French friends about his impending journey home, which gave me an idea. That annoying little magnetic box could work for its living on his vehicle. With my DS out of sight, being safely locked away in its garage, the trackers might be convinced to follow one Opel Rekord saloon to its Lubeck, West Germany, address!

 With the date decided on and my ticket bought, I was left to secure my property before the early morning departure. It was only when having boarded the express train at Bordeaux and sat all alone in a compartment; that all sorts of troubling thoughts came to me. Firstly, how can you trace a man who changes his lodgings frequently, staking out the old ones would be a waste of time? Walking around even a small area of this city, in the hope of seeing a certain person made no sense; while using a bicycle or motorbike to cruise around on wasn't advisable for anyone unused to Paris traffic. Public transport was out of the question, for, if by some miracle I managed to spot my target and he realised there was someone following him, I could be trapped inside a Metro train or on board a bus. No, hiring a small car was the only viable option.
 Further thinking had me mark all my target's previous lodgings on a map of the city, which showed he favoured a particular suburb, maybe there were fellow plotters living close by? Using a different disguise each time, I decided to travel around that area on a daily basis in the hope of seeing him. If all that went well, I was left with one final problem, where to carry out the elimination? This big city was crammed full of people and therefore, busy twenty four hours a day, seven days a week. Sure, at night the place abounded with dimly lit streets and dark corners, but still, the chances of someone witnessing the crime were high. That dilemma stayed with me,

until my train reached its destination.

Safely booked in my cheap hotel and a Simca Aronde hire car at my disposal; there followed long days of observation, which yielded no sign of the elusive Monsieur Firmin. After six days of this routine, I was already considering a different plan of action, but disguised as a young man with long black hair and blue overalls, I ventured forth once again. Using my irregular search pattern, I nearly crashed into the car ahead on seeing my target stood at the roadside, obviously waiting for someone. Pulling into the nearest parking place, but leaving the engine running, I sat quietly observing him in the rear view mirror. When his lift, a Renault Dauphine, finally arrived there was an acrimonious exchange between passenger and driver; oh dear, my target doesn't like bad timekeepers!

They sped off past me, so I followed a discreet distance behind them, intent on discovering their destination. A few minutes on, they occasionally took a left or right turn, to weave through side roads, but always ended joining the original highway. By the time this dimwit realised they knew I was following them, it was too late; their car had disappeared. However, a glance in the rear view mirror told me the hunter had become the hunted, the Renault was right behind me! The yelp of surprise had me race off, eager to avoid any contact; only to run into a traffic snarl up. With no other choice, my car carved a way past, the screeching tyres accompanied by the blare of horns, as I used all the road until abruptly turning right. Hurtling through this back alley, had the car swerving left and right, barely missing the parked lorries and startled workers who were loading and unloading them. Phew, apart from some unheard swear words and shaken fists everything remained intact. Reaching the end, I gratefully exited onto a wider road, where it was time to extend my slender lead; while keeping a lookout for something to reverse my situation. Sweeping past a never ending combination of housing and the occasional area of shops, I was fast losing hope, when a multi-storey car park caught my attention. With a minimal loss of speed and a squeal of tortured tyres my car was steered for the entrance, to hastily collect a ticket, then power away upwards. Knowing that the lower levels would be fully occupied, it came as no surprise that there were no visible gaps until reaching the fifth floor, where the search began for a large vehicle to hide behind. That turned out to be a Peugeot estate car, which had my car parked alongside it in double quick time, ready and waiting for my pursuers to pass by.

When they did, a chirrup from the tyres had me pull out and follow them, determined to keep it that way this time. Now then, let's see what they get up to, with our roles reversed?

Sliding around sharp corners on the slippery surface and rocketing our way between rows of parked vehicles was the answer; then they decided to ascend, where excess speed had both our cars come close to kissing the bare concrete surfaces, until we burst out into the light at the rooftop. While this cat and mouse game continued, Monsieur Firmin produced a gun, leant out of the window and pointed it at me. Dodging behind one of the few parked cars there, I hurriedly pulled the pistol from my bag; then gave chase once more. Strangely, the sight of me also waving a gun around, had my target slide back into his seat, the driver immediately heading for the down ramp at a ludicrous speed.

Back inside the building noise levels increased, the sound of roaring engines and squealing tyres being joined by a metallic scraping as car in front slid off course and came up against an unyielding wall. Rewarded by showers of sparks coming my way, the downward spiral continued with other vehicles being bullied out of the way before reaching ground level. I swear their car was fully sideways as it scrabbled round the tight bend leading to an exit, where it demolished the barrier on its way to joining the avenue outside.

Once among the traffic they exploited every gap, swerving round slower moving vehicles, relying on others to take avoiding action when disregarding all traffic signals; while I kept as close as possible. All too soon we joined a multi-lane highway heading out of the city, where a high speed game of 'chicken' ensued; our unconventional progress past slower vehicles causing noisy indignation from their drivers! Eventually we turned off to enter a bewildered maze of ordinary two lane roads and side streets, which had us hurtling from side to side, narrowly avoiding parked vehicles and pedestrians; heart stopping moments aplenty as we squeezed past with millimetres to spare. Speeding down one straight stretch, actually had other traffic pull over and let us past on the approach to a roundabout; but we soon found out this was no courtesy move. Hitting the greasy surface at speed had both cars out of control within metres, sliding around with steering wheels being wrenched this way and that, while some deft footwork on the pedals was applied in attempts to avoid the kerbs. I don't know how we made it to the turn off in one piece, for both cars were all crossed up as we veered onto the new tarmac surface, swerving violently from side to side as we fought them back to a straight line. Not that any of this had deterred the Renault driver, who quickly regained top speed as we headed for an industrial area.

 This had me drop back, concerned that my target had help available nearby, so proceeding with caution; I looked around, wondering where that might be. We continued on, passing various small factories and then a row of warehouses, most of which appeared to be empty and abandoned. Assuming my target would carry on past them, it took me by surprise when the Renault suddenly swerved to the right and shot inside the last one, having reached the far end by the time I entered the building.

 Next moment a railway locomotive appeared out of nowhere, hitting the car with an almighty bang; the cacophony of hissing, metallic scraping and screeches continuing as the two disappeared out of sight, while the following goods wagons shuddered to an equally noisy halt. Next second, the area lit up as I heard a 'whoomph' noise; some distant siren beginning to wail as black, acrid smoke drifted inside the building.

 I backed out of the warehouse, retracing my route, only to be stopped by some running men.

 "What the hell happened?" their leader gasped.

 "One of our locos had a major problem," was my deep voiced reply. "Now a fire has started, so I have to ….." my explanation left unfinished as they had continued toward the billowing smoke.

 Driving off and eager to get away, I then realised that my disguise could be recognised; so pulling over at a quiet spot, the cap, overalls and black wig were quickly removed. With a rapid application of some make-up and the fair hair brushed, it was enough to gain smiles from anyone I met when motoring sedately back into the city. With my car checked, cleaned and returned to the hire company, I walked back to the hotel, having decided to return home the following day.

The early morning weather turned out to be dull, cloudy and none too warm, hastening my step to enter the Gare d'Austerlitz, where after buying my ticket, I wandered around the concourse looking for a kiosk. With newspaper in hand and curious to know how yesterday's events were reported, I boarded the express train to Bordeaux, settling down in my warm compartment for a good read. Sure enough, there was an article about a railway locomotive hitting a car, the crushed vehicle having then caught fire, resulting in the deaths of its two occupants. There was some speculation, but little explanation as to why the car had strayed into this well-signed and busy goods yard. However, there was no mention of any wild car chase prior to this; perhaps maniac drivers were part and parcel of everyday life in Paris nowadays!

Arriving home, a quick check revealed it hadn't been tampered with, plus those two black boxes mounted in the pine trees had been removed. Could it be I was now considered a trustworthy operative by my anonymous employers; or had some new surveillance toy, been hidden elsewhere within my property. Well, if there was, my two day search failed to find anything; leaving me to ponder, was I really the subject of some insidious, psychological experiment?

Wondering what I could do about these intrusions,

my thoughts turned to the sea; for there would be no cameras pointing in that direction. This foolish woman soon discovered that swimming in the Bay of Biscay is a chilly affair during springtime; so I purchased a wetsuit, along with a snorkel, goggles and fins. This changed everything, the fascinating underwater world opened up a new horizon for me, though the quest to see ever more marine life meant staying in the sea far too long; my shivers continuing long after I returned home. Lord only knows why I rush headlong into everything that pleases me.

CHAPTER NINETEEN
'Nice, Then A New Hobby'
Biarritz, France, 1962

Even in this welcome September sunshine the summer flowers were beginning to fade, but its warmth had me relish these remaining lazy days, wandering round my still colourful garden surrounded by busy insects; only to have one afternoon spoilt by the arrival of two familiar faces.

"Good day, Mlle Bergamont," the talkative one began, having left his companion at the far reaches of the lawn. "You obviously know why we are here; so let's sit down over there, where I will explain your next assignment."

Here we go again, I thought, purposely seating him to face the sun.

"You will be aware of the major projects initiated by the present government, like the aircraft industry, upgrading of the roads and an enlargement of Marseille docks?" which had me nod. "Well unfortunately, organised crime has taken an interest in these too. One particular group is already setting up a protection racket, targeting all transport and material suppliers in the south. While no one must be seen to be overriding the Gendarmerie's authority, my masters are adamant, they will not allow a Mafia situation to develop within this country; therefore, the leader of this criminal organisation is your target."

"Forgive me, but by eliminating the gang boss, it

could lead to worse problems, not solve the existing ones," was my argument against this.

"I have to agree, but this is a risk they are prepared to take. So, with their decision made, you are charged with finding a satisfactory solution," he concluded, leaving me with a photograph and some pages of information.

Well, thanks for nothing, I thought, watching the two men head for the beach access, then disappear from view.

The photograph showed a tall, slim and well-dressed man with blue eyes and grey hair, whose studio pose smile came with a look of surprise. Fifty-two year old Monsieur Claude Mondine, was a somewhat elusive character; born in Marseille to professional parents, little was known about his upbringing, while reports of his voluntary military service with the International Brigades during the Spanish Civil War were similarly vague. He disappeared completely throughout the Second World War, only coming to police attention in the early 'fifties, when arrested as part of the gang who conducted a particularly daring bank raid. However, with no evidence of participation in this robbery, he was released, to sink into obscurity once more.

Only when a whisper circulated the underworld indicating he had taken over leadership of this gang in a bloodless coup, did the police sit up and take notice. This turned into an official investigation several months later, when the deposed man was found shot dead in his home; though again, they found nothing linking Mondine to the murder. Since then, his criminal organisation had grown to become one of the most powerful in the country, though this now wealthy individual is rarely seen in public.

He owns a six bedroom house on hilly ground, inland of Nice, but its high exterior walls and patrolled grounds make it hard to ascertain if he was actually staying there. Security is tight; the staff had to live on the premises, while access is strictly controlled at its gates, though helicopter flights had been seen arriving and departing.

To help in locating this man, I was given the telephone number of a reliable underworld contact. Hmm, let's hope that person's claim is true, otherwise he or she could land me in the worst mess ever! For my own sake, I would also have to visit the local library before leaving home; a little reading was needed to expand my knowledge of another mode of transport.

It was October before I set off, equipped with a fully loaded knapsack and tripod; the hours of hiking around steep hills turned into a test of endurance, until at last, a spot which overlooked Monsieur Mondine's property appeared. This small ledge; shaded by a pair of pine trees clinging to the steep slope behind it, was the perfect place to remain unseen while observing the house and grounds, some two hundred metres away. The rifle was assembled and made ready for immediate use, while my basic camping gear was set up for a few days stay; cold food and drink only, of course.

I didn't have to wait long, for just two days later, the rising sun brought with it the drone of an approaching aircraft, the Alouette helicopter clattering noisily overhead, then circled round to land on a large grassed area within my target's property. Hurriedly putting the tripod in position to steady my view, the binoculars showed me Mondine and three other men had alighted and were making for the house. As all four wore smart suits, it was hard to tell if the visitors were guests or merely bodyguards, so I decided to await developments.

It was almost eleven o'clock before anyone ventured outside, the two bulky figures taking up their positions either side of the house, while the four who interested me, trooped out minutes later. They sat at an outside table enjoying coffee and drinks, their relaxed demeanour telling me these were old friends; oh, to know what they were talking about! Fifteen minutes later they returned inside, having me wait until two in the afternoon before they reappeared. While the helicopter was being made ready for flight, the three guests shook hands with Mondine and were about to make for the machine, when a woman came running out of the house to deliver a message to their host. He listened, then had her run back inside, only to return carrying a briefcase; taking it from her, all four men walked to the helicopter and climbed aboard. Right, too much time has been wasted trying to locate you, Monsieur Mondine, so my task must be carried out now.

The turbine engine whined into life, its rotors beginning to turn as power was increased; while I looked through the telescopic sight at my targets. The helicopter lifted off and was gaining height when my first bullet struck its tail rotor gearbox, while the second tore into the exposed engine's fuel system. Starting to spin out of control, the engine then died, having the machine descend rapidly. Thankfully, it stayed within the boundary walls as it sank down, to land on a large wooden building; but, unable to support this unstable weight, the roof promptly collapsed. Toppling over to one side, it continued down, the fearful racket reaching me as the rotors destroyed themselves and the structure in a maelstrom of smashed wood and metal. Coming to rest on the concrete base, all mechanical components ground to a halt and the debris subsided. There was a second of quiet, before a huge fireball lit up the area, bowling over the bodyguards who had raced to the scene. This ignited aviation fuel from the helicopter's ruptured fuel tank; which combined with whatever was in the building, created a raging inferno, making any rescue attempt a futile exercise. Convinced little would be left of the helicopter, or those inside, before any fire engines arrived, I packed up my equipment and left, heading north over the mountains.

Only later did I realise that while those four human beings were being noisily cremated, many thousands of kilometres away leaders of the world's two superpowers wisely decided millions more wouldn't suffer the same fate. The Cuban crisis was defused, though the Cold War rumbled on.

Back home, I returned to the sea, where the limited range of my underwater explorations were beginning to frustrate me; leading to a decision to try scuba diving. So, with my new 'urchin cut' hairdo and different make up to dampen any security concerns, I headed north to a holiday resort which had dive schools; to foolishly try the first one which appeared. There the handsome, bronzed instructor looked me up and down; then commented.

"Are you sure about this, I would willingly have you take a course, but managing this heavy equipment may be a problem?" a question which immediately had me determined to prove him wrong. Well, I won't deny it was hard work on dry land, but manageable once in the water; which seemed to satisfy him.

"Well done," came as he stared at me. "By the way, haven't I seen you before, you're 'Miss Angel' the fashion model?"

"I wish," came as a suitable answer was sought. "Anyway, that's a sideways compliment, for as you well know, the poor girl died in a tragic accident; though even if she was still alive, you will find I am a considerably older."

"That doesn't make you any less desirable," came as his eyes roamed over my bikini clad body.

"Why thank you, kind sir," was my insincere reply. "A word of advice, more work is required on your courting technique."

Well, surprisingly he did and being a sucker for compliments, I let him take me out to dinner, where he proved to be an amusing and attentive companion. That is, until one drink too many had him change to a rude and aggressive bore. From then on I backed away, eventually changing dive schools to one run by an older man, whose stated mission was to turn his pupils into informed and safe divers, nothing more.

Yves, our instructor, had the same doubts about my strength, but having proved him wrong, the course proceeded apace.

CHAPTER TWENTY
'Old Agent, New Problem'
Biarritz, France 1964

I had expected those on high to keep me busy, but the tasks had been few and far between since being 'recruited' to serve my country; if memory serves me right, Papa was called upon many more times. Maybe it was true, there must be far more renegade criminals than enemies of the state; yet both these troublesome types desire the same rewards, money and power.

Be that as it may, the next appearance of my black suited pair came at an awkward time, for I was cleaning the diving equipment; having to bundle it in the nearest hiding place, the garden shed. Never sure whether they knew what my hobbies might be, it was better not to take chances.

"Good day, Mlle Bergamont, you must know why we are here again," said the talkative one, having left his companion at the beach access. "I bring news of your next assignment. My masters have discovered that an individual has taken undue interest in some of our country's aeronautical projects. Whilst these aren't classified as 'top secret', those on high wish to discourage this kind of interference in our affairs."

"Oh come on, why can't they arrest and jail this person," was my annoyed reply, "the publicity would make others think twice, thereby solving their problem."

"I may agree with you, but as a mere messenger, my opinion counts for nothing," he concluded, handing over a photograph and some notes. With that he left to join his companion, the two of them disappearing via the beach. Still annoyed, I retrieved the diving gear and finished my job, before looking at their paperwork; though the first scan through it gave me an uneasy feeling.

My target, John Bell, aka Monsieur Jacques , was an unremarkable looking man, average in every way, apart from his engaging smile. However, this forty-two year old Englishman had been recruited by the SOE during the Second World War because of his knowledge of France and its language, serving over here before and after the D-Day invasion. Thought to have joined MI6 after the conflict, he disappeared from view until now, being seen in Toulouse recently.

Um, this is the first time I have come up against a trained spy, saboteur and killer, who wouldn't think twice about batting me to oblivion. Disregarding that, the British had their own advanced civil and military aircraft, so what did they actually hope to gain by having Monsieur Jacques spy on our manufacturers? Not convinced by what was in the notes, I was sure some other agenda was being played out.

Using another disguise and driving a hire car, I arrived in Toulouse to make my quiet little hotel a base. Having a list of places Monsieur Jacques frequented, I spent some long, boring hours waiting for him to appear; but, imagine my surprise when he finally entered a cafe with three females. I judged them to be around my age, not the pretty young things middle age men normally go for. Following them inside and sitting close by, the first thing I noticed was, while the ladies lingered over their coffees, he downed four brandies; not a normal person's mid morning thirst quencher. Other than that, my efforts to hear their animated conversation were hindered by the background noise of this popular place, not helpful.

The only alternative was to have him lead me to where he was staying, which he did. Along the way the ladies left his company, but then another appeared; who stuck with him all the way to his apartment, entering it and locking the door behind them. Damn, an early morning stake out beckoned.

Next day, there was no sign of them until late morning, when they left the building, his partner disappearing before he collected two different ladies to have a long, leisurely lunch in the city centre, before wandering back to the same cafe, et cetera. After two days of this, I was confused; did he go anywhere near the airport, no. Did he look as if he ever would, no; so what the hell was going on?

Day three, things changed as the pair collected just one other lady, then headed out of town by car; while I followed them at a discreet distance. Some thirty kilometres later, we had entered a wooded area, where their car turned off down a narrow track. Hiding my car some distance away behind some bushes, I ran back tracing their tyre tracks through the trees till seeing a flash of sunlight on glass. Next moment there was a gunshot, then another; the wild fluttering of birds ending in a nervous silence. Crouched down with my gun out and ready for use, the only movement was a vehicle returning along the track, so I waited till the exhaust noise faded into the distance. Moving carefully forward, I kept going until coming across a woman's body propped up against a tree; she had been shot and left with a notice around her neck saying a name, with 'traitor to France' written underneath.

If this was retribution for some wartime act, why had it taken so long to catch the guilty party and why was an Englishman involved? An anonymous call to the police was made, in the hope of bringing some clarity to the situation. While awaiting the result of that, Monsieur Jacques' apartment remained next day's focus; which turned out to be somewhat different.

At nine o'clock, the pair appeared along with another lady, whose reluctance was visible as she was forced into a car. I guessed correctly that, they weren't going to use the same spot to eliminate this second victim; so their car was never out of my sight, the intention being to stop this madness before it began.

That turned out to be impossible; also the derelict farmhouse they chose had open ground around it, meaning there was every chance my approach would be detected.

"Alright, come out with your hands up, now," commanded a male voice; a bullet in his direction being my answer. "That was a waste, any more silliness and you die a slow death." I don't like being threatened, so a handful of pebbles thrown into the next room was my reply. Two more gunshots had ricochets whining off the crumbling stone walls as I leapt from room to room trying to end up behind my gun toting rival. Rounding a corner to come face to face with his partner, her surprise silenced by my gun barrel before managing to shout a warning. Stepping over her crumpled form, I entered what must have been the kitchen, to see my target stood out in the open, holding his gun to the other lady's forehead.

"Okay, it ends here, put your gun down and show yourself, or the lady dies," he ordered. I had no time to obey, for a loud screech from behind had his bloodied partner rush at me, but my dodge to one side had her trip and fall through the doorway to land in an undignified heap. Two quick gunshots later she was dead, closely followed by Monsieur Jacques, who had faltered upon realising what he had done. Lying in an expanding pool of blood alongside his intended victim, this middle aged woman remained stock still, unseeing but babbling incoherently. Afraid the noise of shooting would attract unwanted attention; I grabbed both arms, talking quietly and calmly to her as we hurried back to my car, pushing the reluctant body into its passenger seat, then drove off to find a roadside stall.

"Here we are," placing a plastic cup of coffee into her still shaking hands. "It will help you calm down." It was a good ten minutes before she realised I had no intention of harming her, asking who I was and what happens now.

"It's better if you don't know who I am, but before being taken home, an explanation of what was going on at the farmhouse would be helpful."

She explained that it all started during early nineteen-forty-four, when Monsieur Jacques had arrived by air to join the local Resistance cell, organising their sabotage plans to coincide with the impending Allied invasion. Unfortunately, months before that took place; the cell was betrayed to the Nazis, having some members arrested and others killed in a dawn raid. The few who survived, including Monsieur Jacques; swore vengeance on the traitor, no matter how long it took to unmask him. Meanwhile, all able bodied men and women in the area had been rounded up by the Nazis and sent to Germany as forced labour; many never returned.

After liberation and Monsieur Jacques back in England, there were many accusations bandied about, but no arrests were ever made; leaving all to forget about the war and concentrate on better things, except for one person.

Lucette Baise, the only member of her family to survive the war, would neither forgive nor forget; forever searching for a person she considered the traitor. Though when she eventually accused this lady's brother-in-law of being the one, everyone laughed and ignored her from then on. Nevertheless, from then on the two families were subjected to a constant cycle of abuse; even after her brother-in-law died.

Things came to a head when Monsieur Jacques returned, for Lucette immediately had him move in with her, where the pair set out to convince others that justice should be done. However, it was soon realised he was a drink sodden shadow of his former self, so there would be no backers for their plan; which must have caused intense anger, for they decided to carry out retribution themselves.

"Dear God, as I know only too well, whatever horrors you have been subjected to, it doesn't entitle you to be judge, jury and executioner, didn't Monsieur Jacques object?"

"No, he was as bad, if not worse than her," she concluded.

I returned to Biarritz still not sure what had been achieved; my only conclusion being that the French and British authorities had colluded to rid themselves of two dangerous individuals, who could have caused more unrest due to divisions the occupation had laid bare. Also, despite reading through several newspapers, there was no mention of any killings at either location; which had me thinking my idea was correct.

CHAPTER TWENTY ONE
'Atomics And Old Boats'
Biarritz, France, 1965

When our president declared France would become an independent nuclear power, complete with all methods of delivering those frightening weapons; the under used armed forces were probably delighted. Elsewhere, most people took a dim view of this proliferation. As for me, well, I knew this would mean more visits from my 'handlers'. Let's face it, the two superpowers knew my country trusted neither of them, so, in turn they would want to know our secrets and intentions. However, as it takes years for a complex project like this to become a reality, I thought an extended holiday awaited me.

 Well, it meant I could pay full attention to my diving course, where Yves was complimentary about my progress; but when it came to extended and deep dives he reluctantly excluded me.
"There is no way you can manage the extra weight safely and I won't take that chance; but you can always stay on the boat with me and learn the duties of a dive master."
Said boat was a wooden ex-fishing vessel, powered by an ancient diesel engine that threw out great gouts of black smoke when in operation, which combined with its well worn paintwork and limited equipment wasn't exactly inspiring me with confidence.

Neither was the so called lesson anything to write home about, for though I was allowed to skipper the boat to his chosen dive site, we sat moored in choppy water, just off the site of a shipwreck, where Yves presented me an instruction book to read. While the other students and instructor had departed in the Zodiac, connected the alarm wire and disappeared under water; I was left trying to read as the boat rocked about non-stop. Ninety minutes of this treatment was more than enough for anyone; but then the divers surfaced and returned to our boat, full of stories about their latest adventure. Back on dry land, Yves told me that next time there would be a test of what I had learnt; though driving home doubts crept in. Sitting around for hours waiting for something to happen, wasn't my favourite pastime; so should I forgo this and try something else? Bereft of ideas, the decision was made to give it another chance.

CHAPTER TWENTY TWO
'Atoms And Oddities'
Biarritz, France, 1966

Well, it had been a while since my two 'handlers' had paid a visit, but when a slight noise had me look up and see them traipsing across my cultured lawn, I ran to the door.

"Next time, would you mind using the path provided," confirming my annoyance, before the talkative one could utter a word.

"Noted, will do," he replied, as I invited him in. "Now then, Mlle Bergamont, my masters have discovered a problem at one of our nuclear research facilities, it seems a high placed member of the personnel is a foreign agent."

"Dear me, I think your employee vetting procedures need to be tightened up."

"No doubt they will be in future," he assured me. "Anyway, this being so, your next assignment requires the elimination of this gentleman, before he has a chance to flee."

"You are aware there is a time honoured and legal way to sort this out; arrest and put him on trial, a guilty verdict will have him in prison or exchanged for one of ours?"

"Quite so, but unlike your previous work, this will also require you to report this gentleman's movements before the elimination," a strange statement with no explanation.

"Sorry, but that doesn't make much sense, you want me to spy on a spy?"

"Come, come, Marie, your talent requires covert observation of a target, does it not?" he reminded me. "Anyway, these will explain everything," handing over a photograph and some typed notes.

With that, he left and joining his silent companion, they walked down the path to my beach access.

According to the notes, my rotund target, Gregori Slovenski, was forty-seven years old and a French citizen, who must have been influenced by Einstein, for he affected the same eclectic hairstyle. This framed his round, rosy cheeked face, which combined with an easy smile and bright eyes, gave him the look of a stereotypical Bavarian or Austrian; but his name suggested East European origins. Though divorced and childless, he was reputed to be a popular figure: who lived in the same block of apartments as many of his single colleagues. A scientist working at one of our nuclear research facilities north of Paris, he was accused of spying for one or the other superpower.

Pardon, you don't know which! What kind of inquiry was carried out before these orders were given? Regardless of what I thought, part of the assignment required me to observe everything during his next visit to Paris, after which a full report would be passed on to the 'handlers'; the elimination was left up to me.

Ahem, Monsieur 'Handler', your notes explained little and merely added to my confusion.

Suspicious of being set up for some unknown fate, my plans were to play it by ear in Paris and act accordingly. Mind you, studying a map of my target's local area, gave me a clue how the end game could be carried out.

 On the appointed day, I parked my hired Land Rover close to the target's apartment block, waiting for his Citroen 2CV to appear. When it did, I followed at a discreet distance, noting his speed and the route taken. Tackling the manic city traffic in such a lumbering vehicle was hard work, but we both arrived near the Soviet embassy in one piece. Parking up, my target headed for the entrance, only for someone to emerge and greet him; an animated conversation taking place as the pair walked off to a cafe, where they sat outside enjoying a coffee. I had followed them, tripping along in my high heels and tight skirt, the only disguise being a pair of oversized sunglasses. Sitting nearby and sipping my coffee, I caught some of their conversation; which seemed consistent to what close friends would chat about. There was no furtive exchange of documents or other such nonsense, so I returned to my hire car and awaited developments. Delving into my large handbag, had an auburn wig, trousers and flat shoes transform my appearance, sunglasses discarded as the sky had clouded over.
 Hurried changes to my make up were finished, just as my target returned to his car and drove off. With the advantage being high up, I managed to keep Monsieur Slovenski's vehicle in sight as we wound our way to the American embassy; where, as before, he parked nearby. There was someone outside the gate waiting for him, only this time it was a woman. Effusive greetings complete, this pair ambled off, arm in arm, without a care in the world, with me trailing along behind them. Visiting a park, they spent time examining the colourful displays of flowers and

watched the antics of various ducks on a manmade lake; acting more like a pair of close friends rather than spies. Eventually our trek ended at a restaurant, where the pair had an extended lunch, as I did. No subtle transfers of documents were observed during their time together; nor romantic exchanges either, they just acted like good friends do. I realise that having contacts from nations that might be considered your enemies was unwise, but that was all this appeared to be; unless those on high knew something I didn't. Good God, did they really consider Monsieur Slovenski was a double, double agent, who somehow extracted or gave away secrets in general conversation! If they believed that lunatic idea, what difference would today's observations make?

Return to our cars was considerably quicker, for the weather had changed to grey skies then rain. Being a savvy lady, I had carried an umbrella, which meant staying dry while my target and his companion were soaked on arrival back at the embassy. The lady received a hurried kiss on both cheeks and rushed indoors, while my target ran for his car; both of us now intent on leaving the city.

Once back into countryside, the downpour increased making travel hazardous; my target having opened his car's side windows to clear the condensation. We carried on till reaching a turn off, which he took, motoring carefully alongside a canal. Following him, but with my lights off, I waited for the left hand curve to come into view, where soft acceleration had his Citroen pushed from behind, till it slid off the road and down an embankment. Entering the water with a splash, its engine spluttered and died, the flimsy bodywork taking on water as it drifted away. Once water reached the open windows it sunk like a stone, leaving just a few bubbles; five minutes passed, but there had been no sign of Monsieur Slovenski, so my work was done.

 Checking the Land Rover for damage, revealed some paint chips on its galvanised front bumper, which were removed before I set off again. Then it was a long overnight journey to return the vehicle to the hirer in Poitiers. Further journeys by train and taxi had me home and to bed, sleeping for many hours.

 My report was collected by just one of the 'handlers', who remembered to avoid the lawn this time; but refused to comment on just what had been achieved.

 Though posted as a missing person, it was some months before Monsieur Slovenski's remains were recovered from the canal; though I never heard of any police inquiry into his disappearance. However, it was noted that his work colleagues organised the funeral; though I doubt there were any mourners who originated from Russia or America.

CHAPTER TWENTY THREE
'Rescue And Thanks'
Biarritz, France, 1967

On returning to my chosen dive school, Yves was remarkably laid back about my lengthy absence from his lessons, saying. "I realise that work must come first for a single lady like yourself; paying for this modern life means sacrifices have to be made," was his considered opinion. This was all the more unusual, because he never asked what I did for a living.

Anyway, I was all present and correct when the next extended dive took place, taking my position on board as we headed for a small, rocky island, several kilometres offshore. With practised ease the students and instructor were kitted out, placed on the Zodiac and taken to the dive site; while I maintained our boat's position, keeping my eye on a distant yacht as it sailed past. Yves returned onboard, with he and I looking westwards at some approaching clouds.

Time passed and the clouds had increased, with rain seen in the distance; while back with us a gusty wind had picked up. Eventually, a now worried Yves called off the dive, long minutes passing as the divers decompressed; the increasing ocean swell having everyone struggle to get back on board. With all accounted for and equipment stowed, I looked around for the yacht; to see its crew struggling to furl the sails. The next moment a violent gust had it heel right over and capsize, having me point and yell at Yves.

"Turn about and head for its position," he shouted back, "Full speed ahead, we have to reach it before it runs aground on hidden rocks off to starboard. Any sign of those on board?"

I shook my head, for inside the cramped wheelhouse, my view was regularly compromised by waves or spray. Nearing the upturned hull, I could make out three figures hanging onto the structure, news I passed on to Yves; as he readied our four best swimmers for a rescue attempt. With his guidance I took our craft as close as we dare risk, where the swimmers began their task. With shouted instructions, the throttle and tiller were in constant motion as I tried to maintain position in worsening conditions. Thankfully, our gallant swimmers and their three lucky survivors were helped back on board before my stamina wilted; though the yacht was last seen drifting towards those hidden rocks Yves had pointed out. As I breathed a sigh of relief and headed for shore, rain began to fall, worsening until everybody bar me was thoroughly soaked yet again.

Back on dry land, the rescued trio, an elderly couple and their grandson, showered everyone with thanks; though the sight of some cameras had me immediately disappear into the background. The last thing I needed was seeing my face plastered all over the newspapers.

"For what you did today, well done," Yves congratulated me, as I prepared to return home. "But be warned, the next time might not be so easy." Is it human nature for people to thank you, then immediately warn of worse to come?

CHAPTER TWENTY FOUR
'Students, Mayhem And Flight'
Biarritz, France, 1968

On a cold and windy afternoon, I was sat in my lounge, busily doing nothing, when the same dark suited man and friend appeared in my back garden via the beach access. Leaving his silent companion to be blown around outside, he was motioned inside to deliver the usual bad news.

"Good day, Mlle Bergamont, you obviously know why I am here. My masters have decided that the growing student unrest in this country is becoming a threat to national security," he announced. "Therefore, it has been decided you will rid us of a leader of this movement and its financial backer."

"Well, the young will always be rebellious because they see things differently, something that our leaders should keep in mind," I replied. "However, the reaction isn't surprising, as this country is run by warmongering old men, who never listen to advice or act on public demands."

"Merely being a messenger, I am in no position to agree or disagree, Marie," was his excuse, handing me some photographs and notes. With that, he left in the customary fashion; while I had a mad thought that those two must be dedicated surfers in their off duty hours!

Examining the photos revealed, Giles Varol, to be a handsome lad, tall, with long, dark hair, soulful eyes and an engaging smile. A third year university student, who was aiming for a degree in aircraft engineering, wouldn't normally be considered a hothead; so, what had this obviously intelligent, but normal individual done to make himself a threat? Protesting that university authorities should treat male and female students like adults, rather than children; was hardly revolutionary!

Then there was his supposed mentor and occasional companion, Raymond 'Big Ray' Osman, a huge, ugly brute, who gave the impression he was the bodyguard, rather than your usual financial backer. A dour looking individual, he definitely lacked that easy smile and air of confidence which all financial whizz kids display to the world. A Communist party member with no university qualifications, he was barely three years older than Giles; which left me wondering if some other agenda was in play here. Giles Varol, do you really know what's going on?

Curious why protesting students were considered a threat to stable government, I read everything available on the subject. My conclusion being, everyone knew the country was run by old men with old ideas, whose authoritarian rule and vast bureaucracy were so entrenched, change was nigh on impossible. Frustrations had been raised, but there was little sign of any insurrection in the making; so were the politicians overreacting, or did it point to something more sinister?

Still harbouring reservations about all this, I nevertheless drove off and headed for Paris, hoping all would be revealed. However, discovering I wasn't allowed to enter the university campus didn't help matters; while hanging around in the cold waiting for my target to show, was more than annoying. Two days later the instantly recognisable 'Big Ray' appeared, walking towards the campus gates, which he passed through without hindrance and disappeared from sight.

My prayers were answered thirty minutes later, when he and Giles returned, striding for the main road, where they hailed a taxi. Hurriedly returning to the Citroen, I fired it up, barging my way onto the traffic clogged highway, intent on following their cab. Keeping a discreet distance behind as it weaved its way through the city to endless suburbs; I soon lost all sense of direction and ended up with no idea where we were. Forgetting about that as the taxi braked to a stop, I cruised past slowly to see my targets alight and head for a row of terraced houses. Hardly had the taxi left the scene when inordinately loud gunshots rang out in this quiet street, the rear view mirror showing me 'Big Ray' had been hit. As he stumbled and fell, an engine roared and more gunshots were heard; the crouched down Giles running towards me, half hidden behind parked cars.

"Get in!" I encouraged, on opening the passenger door. "Now stay down," came as he scrambled on board. He stayed quiet while my pistol was removed from the glove box, both of us keeping low until a large van roared by and turned off at the next junction.

"Who are you?" he asked nervously, staring wide eyed at the unusual looking weapon.

"I was employed by the government to be your executioner, Giles," my answer having his eyes blink in alarm. "But fortunately for you others have the same idea, which changes things, because I don't like being subjected to mixed agendas."

"What about Raymond, shouldn't we call for an

ambulance?"

"I'm sorry to tell you, but our gun-toting friends have made sure your 'Big Ray' is well past anyone's care," was my hurried reply. "Now, it's time for us to depart this place and leave Paris, assuming you know the way?"

I drove off sedately before any concerned neighbours put in an appearance, intent on finding some out of the way place where young Giles could explain what the hell was going on. Telling my fretful passenger we were heading south, he gave quick and precise directions, thus speeding our departure from this over populated area. Unfortunately, we appeared to be heading into some nasty weather, for the horizon was filled with dark clouds, I hoped that wasn't an omen! However, all went well until we joined a national route and settled into a gentle cruise; when coming up behind some slower traffic, a glance at the rear view mirror saw a vehicle in the outside lane rapidly overhauling us!

"We have a problem, that bloody van must have followed us," I announced through gritted teeth. "Someone is obviously still intent on doing my job for me."

Accelerating to the fastest speed possible was of no avail, for the van remained stationed behind us; how was this possible, surely no vehicle of that type was capable of cruising at one hundred and forty kilometres per hour?

"Find me any line of tarmac that looks like a corkscrew," I demanded, passing over my road atlas. "We're never going to outrun that thing, but we might be able to put it in a ditch."

Giles scrabbled through pages showing the area we were in, until tracing one likely candidate.

"I've got it," he cried. "After another ten kilometres turn off and head for Fouget, two kilometres past there, turn right; this road should suit your purpose."

Taking him at his word, I followed all instructions; watching as the 'escort' followed our every move, until at last, we turned onto the one recommended by Giles. This 'road' was really a narrow lane bound by high hedges, barely wide enough for one vehicle, let alone two trying to pass safely.

"Don't panic, this is one way only," Giles confidently asserted. "Actually, it's a private road belonging to a quarry, by which empty trucks return to base; logically, that would happen in the evening. Loaded ones leave, joining it and going the same way, until reaching the main road again."

"I hope you're right," came my reply as we accelerated away, to screech round blind corners at insane speeds, while my navigator shrunk down in his seat. He stayed that way as we floated from one side to the other, with me concentrating like never before, trying my hardest to keep the blue missile between the hedges. A hill loomed in the distance, though, as this lane meandered around every perceived obstruction, it took an age to reach it. Once there, a surprise awaited us, the other side was completely gone, quarried away. Mesmerised by this, I was a teeny bit late noticing a tractor emerging from a field; luckily, a blast from the horn had it stop, thereby averting disaster. This event had my passenger shrinking further back into the upholstery of his seat, a position he stayed in when we came up against a large truck, whose size prevented any dodgy overtaking manoeuvres.

By the time we reached the quarry entrance that blasted van had caught up with us, so in an attempt to outrun it, when there was room to pass our slow moving obstruction, a stamp on the accelerator gave us a clear view ahead. Splashing through multiple puddles of grey coloured sludge, I followed the well-worn track until it suddenly plunged downhill inside the quarry. This enormous, multi-layered hole in the ground was truly awe inspiring; the yellow painted vehicles at the lowest level looking like children's toys. With that damn van no distance behind, I was committed to following the track; so down we went, the Citroen powering round an endless bend, the front tracking true while its rear end slithered from one side to the other. This was better than the vehicle behind us, which was tying itself in knots whenever the driver asked for more speed. It was like taking part in some crazed speedway race; only it would take a terminal accident before my pursuer gave up any chance of winning. Then, despite the obvious difficulties, my worst fears were realised when the barrel of a gun appeared out of the passenger side window and firing began. The tell-tale stutter of an automatic weapon had me try anything to mess up the shooter's aim, every one of the massive dumper trucks we met becoming the ideal, large obstruction; other than that, weaving dangerously all over the track had to suffice. On and on this mad game went until reaching the lowest level, where some deft steering inputs avoided contact with a taped off area and the diggers parked nearby. Groups of yellow coated men turned and looked at us in alarm, just as a huge explosion took place; a whole section of ground by the side of us literally collapsed and disappeared under the ensuing cloud of dust. Stunned and blinded by what had just happened, I was forced to slow down; so, by the time it cleared, the van was rapidly overhauling us again. Slamming my foot down on the accelerator with a vengeance, the furiously spinning front wheels covered all and sundry in a shower of grey gloop as we powered away, searching for a way back up and out of here. Round and round we went, our slender lead increasing after passing several of the lumbering dumper trucks, though when we were clear of obstacles I felt, rather than heard a bullet strike the Citroen. No immediate damage manifested itself, the instruments were all normal, though the car's attitude dipped momentarily.

 Being a reasonable distance ahead of our pursuers, I pulled over and slid to a halt at the edge of the track; leaping out to discover the left rear tyre was punctured. Damn it, I cried, hastily assembling the sniper rifle and making ready. As the van neared, its sliding and slithering progress had their first burst of gunfire way off target; not so mine, which punctured its front tyres. Altering my aim to the windscreen, the explosion of glass silenced any return of fire; though the vehicle kept going on a somewhat eccentric course until teetering on the track's edge. This slowly crumbled away under its weight, having it tip over and disappear from view in slow motion. The sound of crumpling metal was our signal to go, though I kept close to a dumper truck until reaching the top level; to accelerate past and leave the quarry at speed, before anyone could block our escape. Hoping attention was now focused on the demolished van; we carried on, all the time looking for a safe place to do a wheel change. To my relief, a suitable spot was found before reaching the main road; so, pulling over, the suspension was adjusted to 'high'.

"Come on, Giles, make yourself useful," I called, while wrestling the spare wheel from under the open bonnet. My silent, ashen faced companion stirred himself, eventually undoing the wheel nuts. Meanwhile, circling around the car, the only damage found was a single bullet hole, just above the reflector on its left rear wing; hmm, a few inches higher and it would have been curtains for me! A frantic search in the glove box, turned up an old, but intact 'F' sticker, which was used to cover the damage after a quick clean of the area; its positioning looked most odd, but so be it!

Apart from that, my poor car was smothered in a drying grey sludge, some of which still dripped off its underside. As both number plates were unreadable, the only hope was that any witnesses to what happened, could only report it was merely one in a million or so of these cars on the road.

With the spare wheel fitted, we moved off and joined the main road, only to drive into one horrendous downpour, the incessant rain causing a deafening tattoo on the metal body. This was convenient in one way, but staying in the spray kicked up by a large truck for a few kilometres, was better at removing the grey sludge, if not for providing good forward vision!

By the time we reached a roadside stall the rain had calmed to shower mode; while my car had returned to its original colour, well alright, an extremely dirty blue!

"Here you are, dear boy," I said cheerfully, after returning with two coffees and a baguette. "Drink up before it goes cold." As the caffeine had my passenger come alive again, even accepting half of my ham and cheese snack; it was the ideal opportunity for me to find out what the hell was going on.

"Now then, Giles, time for a serious talk. You

already know I was instructed to eliminate Raymond and yourself, but the reasons why are further complicated by all that has happened. Explanations are required, the truth please, or your mortality will again be in doubt."

"The whole protest was basically to encourage some up to date thinking by our strait laced university staff," he blurted out. "We don't live in the nineteenth century; nor are we naughty children, so, just change the rules and treat male and female students like responsible adults."

"This is already known, though I sense there's a 'but' coming,"

"The university refused to do so, so for a while we were unsure what to do next; then I met Raymond," he continued. "He was a devoted member of the Communist Party, who wholeheartedly believed that if we all pulled together for the greater good, there could never be another war. Alright, he wasn't well educated, but his condemnation of the inequalities within our society made sense to me."

"I agree with him, but it's impossible, some people want to lead, while others are content to be led; which causes all the problems we've had to live with since time immemorial."

"Precisely; anyway, a small group within the Party appeared eager to finance and organise larger protests, for they knew of many ordinary people, who also wanted a change from old men and old ideas running the present authoritarian and bureaucratic system. We accepted their help, but larger protests resulted in the university being shut down, which only encouraged the group to organise even bigger protest marches, ones that the government couldn't ignore."

"Are these still being planned now?"

"As far as I know, yes," he conceded. "But a few days back; Raymond recalled a conversation inside the Party headquarters, one that shook him to his very core. Passing one of the anterooms, he overheard the top three of our backers openly discussing a series of bank raids, all timed to take place when the police were busy trying to counter the violence they intended to foment during our march. Contacting an old friend for advice on what to do, we were on our way to see this person, when all this began."

"Would it also shock the Communist faithful to know that a government agent was in their midst; why else would I be involved?" I reminded him.

"No, it would be expected, for they have agents embedded in all other political parties, 'know thy enemy' has been the watchword for many years."

"Well, you live and learn, but one wonders, who watches the watchers?" I asked in jest.

"Probably the Americans, who in their paranoia, accuse all other diplomats of being spies, while theirs are one and the same."

"Careful Giles, remarks like that can get you killed, as you should know by recent events."

"Okay, so what happens from now on, if our bank robber friends don't get me first, I suppose you will?"

"Contrary to what you might think, I have no desire to kill an innocent; but disappearing for some time will be a necessity; do you have a passport?"

"Yes, it's in my jacket, kept there so my parents can't interfere with my movements," he replied candidly. Oho, don't say another word, Marie; families don't feature in your resume.

"Right, the decision is made," I eventually told him. "We are going to Frankfurt airport so you can take a

BEA flight to London; where, as long as a low profile is maintained, it will remain a safe haven.”

“Don’t worry, after all this mayhem, it’s the quiet life for me from now on,” a statement that didn’t really sound convincing.

With that we drove off, heading east, with me contemplating the immediate future; with Raymond, plus several criminals dead and Giles soon to be faraway, surely my mission was accomplished, wasn’t it? I mean, nobody had ever asked for a blow by blow account of any past assassinations. Putting that to the back of my mind, we motored on with my passenger staring vacantly at the passing scenery; perhaps he was already contemplating a bright future in foreign climes.

Entering West Germany via a back road, flashing our passports and car insurance document at the solitary official, had us waved through without stopping, continuing on till finding an autobahn rest house, in which to stay overnight. Hearty meals and a dreamless sleep had us up bright and early, intent on arriving at the airport in good time.

With a seat booked on a mid-morning flight, we wandered around the terminal building observing the comings and goings of civilian airliners and American military transports. However, seconds before there was an announcement concerning his departure gate, Giles passed a news stand full of fashion magazines, where he turned to me with a huge smile on his face.

“That’s it! Ever since we met, I’ve been certain you were familiar, but the name escaped me; however, these photographs brought it all back,” he breathed. “Step forward ‘Miss Angel’ Bergamont, previously a top mannequin for Karsch couturier in Paris."

My instant reaction was to draw him close and give a kiss on each cheek; then I whispered in his ear.

"For your continued wellbeing, it would be advisable to forget any assumptions and erase me from memory. Now go, fly away and concentrate on making your new life a success."

When Giles was out of my sight, I rushed for the nearest toilet, seeking out a vacant mirror. With my fair hair dyed auburn and scrapped back into a ponytail, little make up and unflattering clothes, how the hell...? Driving back home, I spent the entire journey to Biarritz telling myself to be more careful in future, while thinking of more convincing disguises.

Well, despite my questionable efforts, discontent in Paris continued, for striking workers joined the students in huge protest marches. These had the government alarmed, thinking a revolution was imminent; especially on witnessing violent scenes between the police and marchers. Some changes were made and by the end of May, things returned to normal in the capital; however, there were no reports of any bank raids taking place during that period.

CHAPTER TWENTY FIVE
'Sea, Fire And Rescue'
Biarritz, France, 1968

"If you're up for a challenge, my dear, I have just the thing for you," said Yves, as I turned up in time for one of the last extended time dives of the year. "You will be in charge of the final dive for this course, acting as dive master as well as skippering the boat." Well, you know me, I will always rush in where others fear to tread; so of course my answer was yes.

Yves went to explain the dive would take place eight kilometres offshore, where forty metres down on the seabed, a relic of the First World War lay rusting away. This sunken destroyer was reputed to still have live ammunition on board, so exploring this dangerous wreck would be the ultimate test of his student's abilities. If they completed this test satisfactorily, he would sign them off as competent and safe divers, capable of solo or group underwater adventures.

That was two days ago, for now we were now at sea, with me skippering our wooden vessel across an unusually calm ocean; heading for the invisible spot marked on my chart. It was a long voyage, but if my calculations were correct, we should soon be at the dive site. Luckily for all concerned, that was a correct assumption; otherwise the divers would not have stayed underwater for so long. My random scans of the horizon confirmed we were not alone out here, a motor yacht and three sailing vessels were visible, as well as a distant cargo ship; though none came close to us.

Happily, there were no emergencies during the dive, but I began to worry when the time limit of their air supply approached; being greatly relieved when a series of heads popped above the surface. With everyone back on board and their equipment stowed away, I headed for shore; only to hear a loud explosion.

"Over there," my divers shouted, pointing to a rising plume of smoke in the distance, so I adjusted our course and headed for the motor yacht at maximum speed. By the time we arrived, a couple of men were attempting to douse the flames emerging from a gaping hole in its side.

"How many on board?" was my first question as we drew close, "five," came the reply. Before anything could be done, another explosion sent the men hurtling over the side.

"You two, get them aboard now," I shouted at the biggest lads, who complied with enthusiasm. "Right, someone take the wheel and go alongside that boat, I'm going on board to find the others." This had one of the girls replace me, steering with a confidence borne of past experience. Having leapt on board the motor yacht, I headed for the cabin, opening its hatch to find it full of smoke. Two ladies rushed out, retching and coughing, as I demanded to know where the third person was.

"It's my daughter, she's in the forward cabin," one of them managed to tell me. Oh great, with fire now making a deck passage impossible, I would have to fumble my way through the smoke filled interior.

Well, things were bloody hot as I reached the galley, flames now spreading inboard with dense smoke concealing the damage. Ripping open the forward cabin hatch revealed the screaming child, curled up against the bulkhead. I grabbed her, wrapped my arms around the small form; then turned and fled for the stern. The heat was now intense, as we coughed our way past the galley and on through the saloon to the rear deck and fresh air, hardly regaining normal breathing when there was an almighty 'boom'. The world went mad, for we now appeared to be flying, then diving to hit something bitingly cold and everything went black.

I came to coughing up seawater while strong arms held me, hands placed over my breasts as my saviour swam towards our boat, where eager arms hauled us aboard. The young girl was already there along with the four grown-ups, who gazed forlornly at the remains of their motor yacht disappearing below the waves.

"Oh dear, not what a skipper should display," was my inane comment, on realising I was naked from the waist up.

"Your tee-shirt was already smouldering when you appeared on deck," one of the divers hurriedly explained, handing over an oversized replacement. "It must have been ripped off during that last explosion. Anyway, you are very lucky; there are only some minor burns on your back."

Our return voyage was uneventful, though most of the time I was figuring out how to make a quick escape once we returned to dry land. As before, when all the thanks and celebrations were in full swing and the cameras appeared, I slunk away and made a beeline for my car.

"What you did out there was worthy of a bravery award, my dear," with seatbelt on and ignition key in hand, this quiet comment from Yves startled me more than you can imagine.

"Maybe, but please, please keep me out of it," I begged, "if my company ever finds out about this affair, my job will be on the line, the financial implications of that could have me saddled with a lifetime of debt."

"Rest assured, I shall make sure your name is never mentioned," he promised.

The whole rescue effort was reported in the newspapers, but tucked away in the inside pages; which would hopefully condemn it to obscurity. Meanwhile, I stayed away from the sea for a while and concentrated on my home and garden.

CHAPTER TWENTY SIX
'Unemployed, Casino Capers"
Biarritz, France, 1969

After our President resigned in April, it appeared my services were no longer required, for with a new government installed, months passed without a visit from my two 'handlers'; which left me wondering, which previously well-connected security official had decided to recruit me in the first place? Intimate knowledge of my topsy-turvy life was known only to very few, though none had been given the complete picture.

However, that curiosity was forgotten, for there were more important things to think about, like how to continue paying the bills; for my unrewarded, 'working for the glory of France', had cost me dear. Previous savings were now almost used up, leaving the car and beloved villa as my only assets; so with a comfortable life to support, but none of the usual marketable skills, what to do? Well, it didn't take too long to realise that having the necessary small arms experience, an underworld contact and access to a specialised gun-cum-rifle, there was just one lucrative form of employment that was available to me. Yes, my past had reared its ugly head once again, to exert control over my life.

Now, I have to confess to gambling on the odd occasion, but this failing did bring me into contact with a talkative bartender of the casino in Biarritz, whose chatter led to my first contract.

It seemed that a few years back a gang had planned to steal a weekend's takings from his employers; but had been caught red-handed by the police. It was never revealed whether this was by chance, or they had been tipped off; though only two of the gang were caught, arrested and jailed, their leader having successfully fled the scene.

Many months later this gentleman, Robert Leon, was seen in Madrid, where mere weeks later there were reports of a daring heist at a local casino, which netted the thieves a substantial sum; neither culprits nor the money ever being seen again. The police came under fire, for having been informed of this man's previous effort long before the event; he still evaded them and their border checks.

During the year that followed there were more successful casino robberies in Europe, though whether all these were attributable to this gentleman is a moot point, but the daring and violent raid that took place in Rome definitely was. Security cameras picked him out as the literal smash and grab took place; police arriving at the scene just as gang members were attempting their escape. The ensuing shootout ended with one robber arrested, another shot dead, one injured policeman and several damaged cars, but no sign of Monsieur Leon. Despite a major manhunt in Rome and a country wide search the police came up empty handed; but it did persuade casino owners in Europe to quietly put a price on his head. A virtual fortune, my chatty barman informed me: offered to anyone who would rid them of this nuisance.

As this was too good an offer to ignore, a spliced

tape message was relayed to the casino owners in Rome, who agreed to deposit their reward in my newly set up Swiss account; on receipt of that, my search for Monsieur Leon would begin.

Reasoning he would avoid taking on any high profile establishments like those in Monaco or London, I considered Switzerland and West Germany could be lucrative targets, despite having effective police forces. My problem was how to locate him in this large populated area, a question I posed to the friendly barman, who replied it was easy; let the criminal fraternity do it for you. With villains spread all over the continent, there would always be someone, somewhere, who knew where a particular person was.

"So, say you posed as one of his jailed accomplices, you're telling me it would take no time at all to find Monsieur Leon?" I queried in a surprised voice. "No, no, nothing comes that easy in this world."

"I assure it does," he shot back in a hurt tone, "see me tomorrow and all will be revealed."

"You're on," I replied, changing the subject to pleasanter things.

Returning the next evening, I made my way to the bar, where my friend was in the midst of serving others.

"There we are, Madame, one chilled white wine, just the way you like it," came a voice behind me. "That will be one hundred and twelve francs, please." He winked as I turned round and handed over the money, where I noticed a scrappy piece of paper amongst the banknotes on receiving my change.

"Okay, you win, but it will be checked out," was my

threatening whisper, before walking off towards the gaming tables, laughing at the absurdity of it all.

CHAPTER TWENTY SEVEN
'Contract, Money, Then Berlin'
Hamburg, West Germany, 1970

Well, here I am in my rented car, parked some one hundred metres from the given address, awaiting developments. Presumably Monsieur Leon has rented a room, for the house has nothing to say it's a hotel, being similar to those that surround it in this suburb. That curiosity was forgotten when two men arrive at the house, where my target joined them and they walked off. Giving silent thanks to my friendly barman, I follow them at a discreet distance, until we eventually come to a commercial centre, where one man walks off around the back of the shops. Another enters the bank situated in a parade of shops, though Leon heads for an outdoor cafe, to sit down and have a leisurely coffee, while idly watching the world go by. Meanwhile, I spent my time window shopping, while covertly keeping an eye on him. When they join up again there are smiles, then all three head off, eventually seen entering a public library. After waiting around for ages, all three men leave the building and go their separate ways, with me following my target back to his lodgings, where he stayed until dusk. I returned to my hotel confused, the nearest casino was some distance away, yet Monsieur Leon appeared content to while his days away doing nothing; so what exactly was he up to?

Bright and early next morning, here I am again on the same street waiting, which continues until almost midday, before my target finally puts in an appearance. Walking off to the same parade of shops, he joined his two friends for a lengthy lunch, seated by the restaurant's front window. This was strange behaviour for a wanted man, seemingly unconcerned about being arrested; though the only policeman I saw never looked his way. Eventually, the trio finished their meal and walked back to my target's lodgings, where they stayed until I gave up and returned to my hotel.

 Next morning heralded grey skies and a cold wind, so for a change I drove to the commercial area and parked, sure my trio would show up again. Well, two of them did, all dressed for the weather, striding purposely towards the bank; just as a car pulled up in front of it. Recognising the driver, a sudden 'light bulb' moment from stupid here, realised they were robbing the place. Drawn closer by some weird desire, I was rewarded by having a gun poked in my face by one of the balaclava wearing robbers.
"Nobody comes any closer or the woman gets it," was shouted at bystanders as he shoved me and three large bags into the rear seat, the similarly attired others scrambling on board as the car screeched off, rounded a corner and hurtled up to a parked van. Coming to a stop, I was dragged from the car and unceremoniously bundled into the van's load area, along with the bags and a pair of gunmen; both their weapons pointing at me. The van drove off at normal speed and continued on a further fifteen minutes or so, before coming to a halt. There, just as I wondered what happens next, my target's two companions were given a bag; which they took to a nearby Volkswagen Beetle, loaded up and roared away.

"You, in the back of this," ordered the now revealed Monsieur Leon, pointing at an ancient Hanomag van.

"Look," I replied in annoyance, "we could get on a lot better if you stopped pointing that thing at me," indicating the pistol hidden in his jacket.

"Oh, we have a feisty one, we'll see about you later." Secured inside the van, we drove off, its speed showing the mechanicals were in better shape than its tatty exterior. The journey was shorter this time, ending after we turned off to enjoy a bumpy ride to somewhere. Released, I looked around at a decrepit wooden structure, its interior being no better, where pushed into the tiny kitchen, my orders were relayed.

"Now you're around, make yourself useful, a meal would be nice," along with pawing at my boobs.

"Look here," was my angry response, "if you want us to get on, can we at least do it conventionally; you find the wine and I will do the cooking, after that, well who knows?"

To my surprise, there was no argument, threats or attempted rape, he just nodded and backed off with a bemused look. A further surprise, the refrigerator was well stocked, leading me to ask the obvious question.

"What's your favourite meal?"

"Wienerschnitzel, sauerkraut and chips."

"Unusual choice for a Frenchman," I exclaimed. "Don't look at me like that; your accent was the giveaway."

"Yours too," he concluded.

Well, with the meal consumed and wine drunk, the amorous advances began; ending with frantic undressing and coupling. I hate to say it, but he was an excellent lover, all my wants and desires were fulfilled, so much so, a repeat performance followed.

Now all sweaty and exhausted, he rolled off me gasping for breath, to receive a pillow over his head. Expecting a fight, I held it down tight, but his body just convulsed twice then lay still. Not sure what happened, the pillow stayed in place for a few moments longer; lifting it off revealed he was indeed dead, a heart attack, maybe?

Now the hard work began, removing any trace of my presence in this shack; it took a strip wash and several hours of non-stop work until I was satisfied. Taking the towel and soiled sheets, they were placed onboard the van, before I drove off in the darkness to find a large rubbish bin; eventually locating a group outside a silent factory. With my detritus mixed in with some other vile smelling residue, the van was directed back towards Hamburg, to be left abandoned at the first S-bahn station it came across. There I had plenty of time to make myself more than presentable; then await the first train into the city centre.

On arrival at my hotel, there was just enough time for a quick breakfast, before paying my bill and rushing off to reclaim the hire car; then it was off to the airport, where the car keys were handed back and I headed for the departure lounge.

I barely remember the take off from Hamburg, so it was no surprise a stewardess had to wake me when the aircraft was approaching Tempelhof airport; no matter, the taxi driver transporting this yawning passenger to my hotel in Charlottenburg didn't complain.

Next morning, despite the grey skies and icy wind, I was raring to go again, venturing out to see all the sights of West Berlin, which of course included a visit to the infamous Wall. Peering through the

Brandenburg Gate at the east, I was overcome with feelings of unease and sadness for those trapped there; the weather must have agreed, for soon afterwards it started raining, becoming heavier as I ran for any cover available.

CHAPTER TWENTY EIGHT
'British Blackmail, Hippies And Banks'
West Berlin, Germany, 1971

Exiting the nearest U-bahn station to my hotel onto a rain drenched street, the umbrella went up as I hurriedly crossed over; before the pedestrian sign added red to the reflected kaleidoscope of garish neon. Slowing to an amble, it was then two men moved up alongside me; just as a car pulled over. Next moment, I was bundled into its rear seat and we took off in a hurry, our driver wending his way from the centre of town to some unrecognised suburb, where we cruised along in silence until turning onto a driveway. The garage door in front of us magically opened, closing immediately after the car was safely inside; but not before I noted the attached house was a substantial, well maintained example of post-war building. Escorted inside, we passed several nicely decorated and furnished areas until confronted with a closed door. My silent companions opened it and pushed me inside, to be left alone in a room full of comfortable looking seating and subdued lighting.

"Ah, good evening and welcome, Miss Bergamont, my name is Connel Dannet," a cultured English voice began. "Before we get down to business, may I offer you a cup of coffee, tea or something stronger?" A question which had me turn, to face an immaculately suited, older man, whose greying hair and benign expression gave him that doting father look.

"A café au lait would be nice, thank you," I replied, having him pass on the request by intercom. Indicating for me to sit down, we waited quietly for a knock on the door; when a loaded tray arrived, complete with a delightful aroma of freshly ground coffee beans. Only after we had tasted our drinks, did he begin.

"Now then, I hope you will forgive the cloak and dagger method involved in getting here, but an argument out on the street, would be both demeaning and inappropriate for all concerned."

"Well, being abducted by strangers is hardly a better way, especially in this city."

"Quite, but Marie, if I may call you that; you and I both know a normal invitation would have been rejected out of hand," he explained.

"So, to what do I owe the pleasure of this enforced get together, Mister Dannet?"

"A long buried file has revealed you are uniquely qualified to solve some problems we have. Ones that we have to be rid of before those on high, both political and military, realise it."

"And if I refuse?" I ventured, knowing full well what the answer would be.

"That would be a foolish decision, for full details of lamentable wartime events in Ardennes, France, will reach the European newspapers; with inevitable results," the voice sounding apologetic.

"Christ, here we go again, history repeating itself," I muttered tiredly. "Officially sanctioned blackmail from my own country's security services had me forced to carry out murderous acts on their behalf. Not only that, it was abundantly clear once my usefulness was at an end, this 'Angel' would be discarded like some piece of trash."

"Alas, nobody remains indispensable in this game," he commiserated.

"That's as maybe, but, are there any benefits for me in your grubby little deal?"

"Of course, Marie, we aren't total monsters you know. When the time comes, a happy retirement will be made available, in a place far from the madding crowd," he stated, smiling to himself.

Not sure what to make of that last comment, but realising his blackmail left me with no other options, I conceded.

"Alright, you win, so what does this 'task' entail?"

"Information from an impeccable source on the other side of the Wall, has told us of an agent sent to the West many years back," Dannet intoned. "Unbeknown to all, she secured a secretarial position in NATO headquarters, though several promotions now have her as personal assistant to a senior American Army commander."

"Oh dear, red faces all round!" I commented. "So, why not get our friends from across the pond to do their own dirty work, they seem adept at assassinating anyone perceived to be a problem?"

"Good God, never!" he shot back. "Our continuing operations here are in a precarious state as it is, without having any Wild West antics upsetting the apple cart! No, though time is not on our side, this task will require considerable forethought and subtlety; qualities sadly lacking in Americans."

"Forgive me, but it sounds as if the Yanks don't even know about this agent."

"Quite so, my dear, but by solving this issue, it might earn us some much needed brownie points; to atone for past errors of judgement, you understand," words that had me picturing Fuchs, Burgess, Maclean,

Philby, et al. With that, he passed over a photograph, which had the conversation peter out as I studied my target and the neatly written biography.

Fraulein Ulrika Kunst, if that was her real name, was a tall, fair haired, thirty-eight year old lady of average build and moderate prettiness, attributes which combined with known secretarial and social skills, no doubt made her the ideal assistant; perhaps a lover too? That thought could make for an awkward situation, especially if they stayed together for the duration of their visit here; I needed my target to be alone for a successful elimination. After some more questions and answers, our conversation ended and a taxi was called; with the perfunctory goodbyes said, it took me back to my hotel, a welcome brandy and bed.

Next morning I was up bright and early, being the first to arrive for breakfast; giving me enough time to purloin a suitable knife from the cutlery tray. As the American General and his staff were due to arrive at Tempelhof Airport before midday, the priority was to hire a car, drive there, then find a parking place from which to monitor the arrivals. As it turned out, my waiting period was cut short when a large American military car arrived in front of the terminal, closely followed by a group of uniformed figures emerging from its doors. As the visitors halted to look at their new surroundings, I noted the conservatively dressed, personal assistant stood close by her much decorated General and his aide. Following a short conversation and a flurry of salutes from the welcoming committee, these three were driven away; while my car followed their transport at a discreet distance.

My target and her two companions were staying at a

central hotel, which was awkward, as finding a parking place from which to observe their comings and goings, was next to impossible. However, after circling round the block several times a car was observed leaving my favoured area, so I shot into that vacant spot at speed, accompanied by a blaring horn ; oh dear, one annoyed motorist, caught napping while intent on doing the same thing!

 Glad to be wearing flat shoes, jeans and a loose top, not forgetting my long, silky scarf; I settled down for a long, but hopefully comfortable wait. Well, there were no movements until after dark, when the aide, now in civilian clothes, left the hotel; striding away with the confidence of someone who knew where they were going. Another hour passed before my target appeared, looked around, then strolled off in the opposite direction to the military man. I followed Fraulein Kunst, curious as to where she was going, for we left the bright lights behind, taking a series of backstreets to a place where loud, psychedelic pop music was being broadcast.
 Good grief, between two windowless concrete edifices, this dimly lit, weed strewn plot was being used for some kind of hippie convention, complete with displays of anti-Vietnam war and 'ban the bomb' placards! The place was heaving with brightly dressed, long haired men and women, most of who merely swayed to the music, puffing away at cigarettes under a thick cloud of sickly smelling smoke. Others were quaffing prodigious quantities of alcohol, while the hardened addicts sat in huddled groups preparing their preferred narcotic.
 Hoping to blend in, my scarf quickly became the regulation headband, while the colourful top was fully

exposed and left unbuttoned, leaving me to drift around unnoticed in search of my target. Carefully stepping around the odd group of candles and abandoned hypodermics, the germ of an idea had me pick one up, along with a discarded cigarette.

 A few minutes later my target was spotted, standing to one side in front of some bushes, giving me the impression she was waiting for someone. Sure enough, some minutes later a man in dark clothing emerged from the shadows, to have my target remove a small package from her handbag. A few words were exchanged on receipt of it, only for him to quietly disappear again; hmm, yet more military secrets handed over to the other side?

 "Got a match, sister," I drawled, on sidling up to Fraulein Kunst, who looked down at me in disgust, but, she handed over a Zippo lighter.

 "Thanks man, you wanna drag, its top grade Mexican," proffering the cigarette.

 "No, thank you," she replied primly, her last words before my two knife thrusts had both of us collapse to the ground, prompting me to giggle when struggling to get up.

 "Hey man, like wow, this stuff is gold standard," I told those nearby, holding the hypodermic up. They merely nodded mechanically; then returned to their own particular narcotic nirvana, while I staggered away until out of sight.

 Hurriedly adjusting my clothing and hot footing it back to the car, I drove back to the hotel; there to have a shower and wash away any hint of drugs. The soiled knife was given a thorough scrub, ready for its return to the dining area, while the clothes were ripped apart and made ready for disposal. That done, I

stood looking at a mirror, talking to my reflection about the evening's events, the considered opinion being.
"Well, Marie, that was hardly subtle, nor was any forethought applied; but so be it, being presented with an opportunity, I just took it!"

By morning, the West Berlin police had issued a statement concerning an unexplained death, which had occurred during the previous evening at an illegal gathering, near the Wall. Evidence of illegal drugs and their use, meant that all the participants had been detained for questioning. I confess to not hearing this first hand, being eighteen thousand feet up in the sky and well on the way to Schiphol Airport, Amsterdam, when the report was broadcast. However, I neither heard nor saw any further mention of this event, so presumably the authorities in West Berlin and their NATO allies had quietly forgotten about it.

Satisfied all had gone to plan, I returned to Biarritz; to find a letter in my post box; informing me a sum of money had been deposited in a bank account in Switzerland. Nonplussed for a moment, a realisation then came to me; the account was Papa's nest egg, which had lain dormant and forgotten in Geneva bank since before the war. My gratification soon changed to horror; those bastards in London must know every detail of my life, but how?
It was bad enough being blackmailed by your own country, let alone another; how many more were lining me up to do their dirty work? God, I should have taken note, Papa always warned me that governments all over the world counted on the ends justifying the means; so long as there was someone

else to take the blame if things went wrong.

Besides that, this 'payment' threw up yet another problem, how on earth was I going to access the funds in that Swiss account? Papa had been a foreigner who lived in France, at a place which now no longer existed; facts that weren't going to help my cause. Plus, official confirmation that a SS major was responsible for his and my mother's death; wasn't something that would be recorded, surely?

Well, there was no other way but explain my situation at the Ardennes district headquarters, where a clerk wrote down all the information I could offer; leaving me to await the result.

The answer came just two weeks later, official, back dated certificates arrived, along with photocopies of existing wartime records, which stated my already injured parents had been arrested in December, nineteen-forty-three, they later died when in Wehrmacht custody. The one and only time I would thank the Nazi's obsessive bureaucracy, if not the accuracy of their information!

All well and good, but now for the second part, would the Swiss bank accept the fact that as Papa's only offspring, I should inherit the money they held for him? Pointing my DS in the direction of Geneva, was the first part of becoming somewhat richer; for on arrival there and allowed into the hallowed portals of this bank, the gentleman who dealt my enquiry soon had his minions scurry away to search through pre-war papers. Returning with the correct documents, they were handed over and examined at length; then all relevant details were cross checked.

"I have to tell you, Mlle Montagne, that everything is in order," he said finally. "In accordance with the terms agreed when this account was set up, your father included a proviso that in the event of his death, said account was to be transferred to your mother, Juliana Legrand. Should she also be deceased, it would automatically become the property of his only child, Marie Angelique."

 Unfortunately there was also some bad news; during the war, communication between bank and client was thought to be ill advised, while letters sent after the hostilities were returned unopened. Further enquiries by them revealed what I already knew; the Nazis had wiped the village off the map, along with its population. This being so, in accordance with their company rules, the account was termed moribund and taken off the active list of investments; meaning the balance hadn't grown at all since then. However, it was still a substantial amount, which I could add to; better late than never to start my personal pension plan!

 On leaving the bank, my relief was palpable, while the weather matched this mood; encouraging me to relax and enjoy the moment. I found a café at the lakeside, ordered a coffee and sat gazing at the scenery. It was then an unusual English pop song was played over the loud speakers, having me listen intently to the lyrics; for it was almost as if the composer had been looking over my shoulder, many years ago. At the end, as the jaunty tune faded away, I shivered, for 'Where do you go to, my lovely', had brought back memories of my time in Italy and the early days in France. Deeply buried emotions rose to the fore again, having me burst into tears; which had a concerned waiter rush to my side, though the garbled explanation probably meant nothing to him.

CHAPTER TWENTY NINE
'Planes, Trains And Agents'
Biarritz, France, 1972

I have to admit the only place to relax, reflect on my life and any future options is at home, where distraction free and curled up on the sofa, one can think things out. However, it is also where the occasional black tide of depression washes over me, fully aware past deeds mean those in power have trapped me in a cycle of organised killings; that will only end with my demise. This abuse, plus the loss of nearly everything that was precious to me, has left only a successful assassination to give any source of satisfaction; a totally illogical sense of revenge, if you like.

Then there are more sensible thoughts, recalling the unpaid 'work' for my country, where most of the victims committed simple mistakes which hastened their eventual demise. Mind you, they were no worse than my blundering around whilst in the Resistance, when only luck and good fortune had kept me alive. Furthermore, they were mainly straightforward eliminations, a single target and no other hidden agenda; unlike the present situation.

Recent cosy, fireside conversations with my British employers were taking a darker turn, where the ultimate goal was becoming more and more obscure. For a small outpost of British Intelligence based in

West Berlin, whose claimed purpose was to monitor civilian and military machinations of those on the other side; surely all resources would be concentrated on protecting their sources of information; namely, agents embedded within the East German establishment? Maybe they were, but a short list of politicians and others, had suddenly appeared. The ever devious Mister Dannet eventually revealed they had become 'persons of interest'.

Good grief, the Soviets were no fools, even if these people were to be targeted and it was possible for me to eliminate some, their reaction would be instant, plunging the world into another Cold War crisis. Dismissing that idea as madness, I wracked my brain for the true purpose of this hidden agenda and more importantly, my expected part in it; but nothing made any sense, so just what the hell was going on?

Then the final shock, my instantly recognised next target, Horst Melke, a charming and interesting person I had met before. This senior manager of some important facility in Chemnitz, he had been one of the guests at a businessmen's get together in Berlin intended to foster better East/West relations; which my British employers had pressured me to attend. With their involvement, I considered it more of an exercise to suss out the opposition! However, Herr Melke and I whiled away our time together, chatting about many things, while carefully avoiding subjects like work or politics. It would have been enjoyable if his two shadows hadn't hovered close by, no doubt ever ready to intervene if the conversation veered from the banal. Still, it was a nice interlude in an otherwise boring evening.

Now though, to have him presented as a target for

elimination, my employers obviously considered he was up to no good; as did the Americans, who had tried to stop the visit.

However, the French authorities allowed it, eager for any trading opportunities; though even their security people were interested in the reason for his unusual travel itinerary. Flying from West Berlin to Paris for talks with the business community, thence by train to Toulouse, where further talks were scheduled: eventually returning by air to Dresden.

Okay, to benefit his electrical company, some focus may be centred on the high speed railway system the SNCF were developing, or perhaps more importantly, advances in radar technology. My employers agreed, but were also convinced that while on the rail journey he would have a clandestine meeting with members of the DDR Intelligence service, relaying some urgent top secret instructions. I considered this improbable, apart from being an unusual and risky proposition, the DDR already had an unbreakable code with which to contact their agents, the numbers broadcast daily all over Europe; eliminating the need for any face to face contact. However, it was made clear to me, the target was to be terminated before any such meeting took place.

It was obvious to all that my only chance of success would be to eliminate the target whilst he was on the train; but, with the deed done, how was I to evade his two minders, plus unknown others and escape undetected? Was this some kind of sick joke, to be stuck on a train, the very situation Papa had constantly warned me against doing?

Left with no choice, my first vague thoughts were that the target must die before the train we were on reached the first of its scheduled stops; at least that offered me the chance of escape after it had come to a halt at the station. So, with little time left, I planned my operation in meticulous detail; though knowing things can and will go wrong, there was a plan 'B'. A very simple one: for my continued existence and completion of the task, it would require quick thinking and improvisation.

Confident my now auburn hair, matching fashionable spectacles, smart suit, sensible shoes and large handbag had me as a travelling business woman; I arrived at the Gare d'Austerlitz early in the morning, even though my tickets were bought and paid for. Boarding the train, to sit in my compartment, stifling the occasional yawn while idly watching as fellow passengers passed by my window; that is, until Herr Melke and his team appeared, where they were given a low key, but official send off.

We departed on time, but my hunger had to wait until the endless suburbs of Paris faded from view, before considering a trek to the restaurant car. Passing my target's compartment and noting he was examining some drawings with a colleague, I avoided the stares of his ever present minders.

After enjoying my leisurely breakfast, reading a newspaper and some aimless gazing at the landscape; it was time to put my plan into action. Winding my way along the corridors I jinxed past occasional smokers or otherwise bored passengers whiling away the time; until, good grief, there just mere metres in front of me stood the unaccompanied Herr Melke about to enter a toilet: unbelievable!

This 'once in a lifetime' chance could not be wasted, so the silenced Berreta was aimed at my target from within the handbag; two near silent shots had him staggering as he was pushed inside the cubicle and its door closed. Next moment, two boisterous children barged past me, laughing as they went; I followed in pursuit of them, hoping my annoyed mother act was convincing when passing my target's compartment.

The train began to slow as I rescued my suitcase from the empty compartment, having me also rush to the toilet; emerging minutes later as an overdressed, grey haired old lady, with a bad attitude. First to alight when the train came to a stop, I immediately harangued a nearby porter to carry my solitary case across to another waiting train, pointing the way with my walking stick. Behind me there were indications of a disturbance, raised voices and the sirens of approaching police cars; while my startled porter received a generous tip as I settled back, alone in my new compartment. The northbound train moved off smoothly, leaving me to glance back, joining worried looking station staff watching the arrival of blue uniformed Gendarmes. Off this train at the first opportunity, I opted for a hire car and the speedy return to Biarritz; never had I been so relieved to be home, must be getting too old for this malarkey!

A letter came after the furore over Herr Melke`s death had died down, my account in Switzerland had been credited with another substantial amount. Included was a note containing the CV of Major Stanislav Vyshinski, aka, Horst Melke. Formerly an electronics engineer and noted linguist, living in Kiev, after being recruited by the Soviet Air Force he was sent to a factory in East Germany, where he headed a team developing advanced electronics, using their expertise supplemented by information stolen from Western companies. Their latest product was new generation, sideways-looking radar, designed for fitment to high speed, low flying aircraft and future missiles; this hi-tech unit was already causing concern in NATO circles.

 Oh dear, poor old Stanislav had been too clever for his own good; but it was curious why an East German facility was used by his team. It was well known that all top secret military research in the USSR was normally carried out at undisclosed locations under total KGB control.

CHAPTER THIRTY
'History Of Lies'
Biarritz, France, 1972

I think most people were cautiously optimistic when hearing the detente between East and West Germany, had resulted in improved diplomatic relations, plus some restrictions on trade and travel were removed, amongst other things. From my point of view, would this also bring a halt to my 'tasks'; somehow I doubted that would happen any time soon. However, the visits from Mister Dannet were a lot less frequent from then on.

 The following year both countries joined the United Nations, though because memories of the recent past were still raw in many other countries; it meant their vocal contributions were considered, but never controversial.

 Then in nineteen-seventy-five the unbelievable happened, East Germany recognised the human rights of its citizens.

 "That's a bare faced lie," commented Mister Dannet in disgust, "the whole country is totally controlled by the state security police, this 'Gestapo on steroids' will ensure the slightest indiscretion will have you imprisoned, interrogated and tortured with no access to any rights, human or otherwise."

CHAPTER THIRTY ONE
'Diving, Death And Mystery'
Biarritz, France, 1976

For years now I had continued scuba diving, guided by a chart Yves had given me on completion of his training course. This treasured possession plotted every rock formation and shipwreck available within the range of my single air supply; more than enough variety for the few hours I could spare for this hobby. In the cause of anonymity, these solo dives always started from the beach in front of my home, where the gently sloping sand made entry and egress from the sea easier.

On this particular dive I decided to explore a rock formation near the limits of my chart, so a gentle swim to and from it was advisable to conserve the air supply. All went well as I submerged, settling into a gentle pace, one which was approved of by the various fish who accompanied me. Some fifteen minutes later and arriving at a well worn, multi coloured mass of rock, I looked around to find myself alone for once. Not for long though, as all of a sudden, something large and grey shot past in front of me, nearly having me lose my mouthpiece, then another and another, until there was a small pod of dolphins swimming around me. They seemed intent on directing me to somewhere, so I followed, but too slowly for their excited ducking and diving. Eventually we reached a wall of broken, brown coloured rock, where one dolphin literally pushed me towards an odd looking patch of black. Swimming towards it I sensed something wasn't right, for it moved awkwardly with the tide; not only that, a quick look back confirmed my companions had also disappeared. Drawing close, I recognised it as another diver, one whose flippers were trapped by a crack in the rock; closer examination revealed the person was obviously dead. Not only that, the air delivery valve was shut off, very odd. With no sign of anyone else around, curiosity had me lift up the face mask, to nearly spit my mouthpiece out, for it was someone I recognised straight away, Giles Varol! As rigor mortis hadn't set in yet, he had died recently; but, without thinking I decided to slowly surface, where, staying close to cover, a detailed survey of the bay in front of me was carried out. Luckily, no people or vehicles were seen or heard during that time, so I submerged once more and headed for home.

There was plenty of time to think on that return journey, wondering about what had happened; for in all probability I narrowly missed witnessing a murder. One where others held the victim down, turned off his air supply, then secured the body to surrounding rocks. Following on, there were my questions; why had Giles returned to France and what criminal activity was he mixed up with? I say this because every bit of his diving gear, down to the smallest component, was matt black in colour. No regular diver would do that, for it pays to be seen, especially in an emergency situation.

In the following weeks and months the newspapers were checked for any articles concerning what I had witnessed, but there was only one in a local offering; which reported the murdered Giles, still in his wet suit, was found washed up on a beach not far from where I saw him. Alarmingly, this article stated that the authorities in Paris were helping the local police with this inquiry; help, how long would my part in his life stay unknown and forgotten? A suspicion that this episode was somehow connected to my working for a foreign power had me on edge for many months, but no one came to arrest me; perhaps British Intelligence won that argument? Nevertheless, it was enough to have me give up diving altogether and turn to an alternative hobby.

CHAPTER THIRTY TWO
'Political Games, Accidental Death'
Biarritz, France, 1981

It was a serious looking Mister Dannet who visited me on this glorious summer's day, waiting till after we were seated outside; before delivering the bad news.

"A dangerous situation is developing on the other side of the Wall," he informed me. "We have been informed that two senior politicians over there, Messrs Voss and Baumann, are trying to convince their leaders that the Americans are planning a pre-emptive strike against the Communist bloc. They claim agents embedded in the West German Army have seen documents which contain plans for one."

"I hope that isn't true."

"Don't be ridiculous, my dear, though the U.S. Army concede to having plans for every possible scenario, even their most gung-ho military types admit that, any such attack would end in a nuclear apocalypse," he countered. "However, that hasn't stopped those two Eastern types from actively pressuring their bloc to act first."

"My God, are these people mad, do they actually want the world to go up in flames?"

"I sincerely hope not; we consider it's more likely to be a political game, both Voss and Baumann seem intent on removing the present leaders and grabbing power for themselves. They also claim, quite rightly, that the old guard seem incapable of stemming the country's economic decline."

"But why are those two stirring things up now?"

"Why indeed, with Soviet attention taken by their war in Afghanistan and the faltering economy, East Germany is also suffering; so it's hardly the best time," he agreed. "This is what makes it alarming, one false move by either side could cause, well God knows?"

"Come now, Mister Dannet, you haven't come all the way here just to tell me this; you have a solution in mind?"

"Correct my dear; an impeccable source has given us a name, Lt Gerhard Linz, of the West German Army, presently serving at N.A.T.O. headquarters," he stated. "This young officer is due to go on leave in a fortnight's time; we need you to ensure he doesn't return for duty, due to some unfortunate, but fatal accident. I stress, his demise must be officially declared as accidental death."

After giving me a photograph and some notes, Mister Dannet said his goodbyes and left; where I noticed the moment my front gate was closed, a nondescript car appeared out of nowhere, in which he departed.

Studying the notes I was given, they told me the unmarried Lt Linz, was a stocky, twenty-six year old of athletic prowess, who was also a keen driver. There was one person he would always visit when on leave, his older sister, Ilse. She lived in Hannover, working as a political journalist, but regularly flew to Berlin on various assignments. Mister Dannet's people were convinced she was his link to the East, but this was as yet, unproven; so why mention it, dear sir?

Linz also had one companion I should avoid, Gustav

Kramer, the son of a high ranking East German military man. He had been arrested some years back for repeated open criticism of the regime, but somehow avoided the usual punishment; instead being exiled to the West, where meeting up with Linz, the two became firm friends.

A fairy story for the uninitiated, though reading between the lines, it was obvious all three were enemy agents who reported solely to Voss and Baumann; but, did it mean documental proof of this supposed pre-emptive strike was already in their hands? Well, it was doubtful Mister Dannet would ever reveal more, so I concentrated on Linz.

Hanging around outside the N.A.T.O. headquarters soon told me Linz and his superior, a huge black, much decorated, American Colonel, were desk bound; their staff car only leaving the base once or twice a day. More important to my plans was the fact, when Linz was off duty, he drove around in a green 'seventies Opel sports car. However, because he lived in the officer's mess, my only chance to 'modify' this vehicle prior to him going on holiday was, if somebody off base warranted a night time visit. Unsurprisingly, that person turned out to be Kramer; who needless to say, was of no help at all, as he lived in a well lit neighbourhood; so I gave up on that.

Dithering around was no help to my dilemma, where all sorts of scenarios were thought of, then discarded as unworkable; until it was too late, Lt Linz was on leave from the following morning. Up early and parked near the Headquarters entrance, I had my hired Mercedes follow his car after it emerged through the gates, going straight to where Kramer lived. He was already at the kerbside ready to be picked up, but instead of heading out of town they drove into town, ending up at the railway station, where Kramer leapt out, to be given a small, round canister. There were hurried goodbyes, then the Opel headed for the autobahn; where upon joining it, his speed increased markedly. Soon we were in the outside lane hurtling along at one hundred and sixty kilometres per hour or more, slower vehicles moved out of the way by a flash of his headlights. I was soon in trouble, for unused to high speed on a crowded highway, mine naturally dropped and he drew further and further ahead; things only changing when we cleared the built up areas and the traffic thinned out. In an attempt to catch up, my car was pushed up to its maximum speed from then on: well, until signs warning of road works ahead appeared. I caught a glimpse of the green Opel up ahead, signalling to enter the slow lane, a forlorn hope because the trucks inside of him were nose to tail and in no position to give way. With the brake lights ablaze but still carrying too much speed, it ran out of carriageway, red and white plastic flying in all directions as the car scattered a regiment of cones, before launching upwards over a pile of broken concrete. Still airborne, loud contact with the highway constructor's large, yellow earth mover had it spin round, clear the median and crash land right in the path of oncoming traffic; where I heard rather than saw further collisions.

 Having no choice but to carry on, I turned off at the next junction to consult my map, finding a minor road that led back to the accident site; using this for a speedy return, my car joined the gaggle of badly parked vehicles, having me walk across a field to join the group of subdued onlookers.

The scene in front of us was lit by a sea of blue and red lights, the police and emergency vehicles surrounding several crashed cars, one badly damaged van, and a large articulated truck with still smoking brakes. Some casualties were already being hurried to a waiting helicopter; while the Opel's mangled remains were being pulled apart to reach the occupant, though the frantic activity stopped when they did. With the helicopter and ambulances gone, photographers finished their work; then accident debris was cleared away allowing the autobahn to be partially reopened. I stayed on until an anonymous black van arrived to collect a body bag, confirmation Gerhard Linz had died at the scene.

Shaken by what the results of speed can do, I rejoined the autobahn, travelling at a modest rate until pulling in at the first available rest stop; where a coffee and brandy had me calm down. I know, I know, but the need was great. Anyway, whilst there one of the staff was caught giving me the eye, for which he received a gentle reprimand.

"But Madame, you are such a pretty picture; all made up and dressed nicely, which you display with effortless style and grace," he replied seriously. "Once I used to see many like you, but alas, nowadays most ladies are uncaring, slopping around in trainers and shell suits."

This made my day, having me stay in a good mood throughout the long journey home: where one week later a familiar letter told me that the usual sum had been added to my account in Switzerland. Such a large reward for doing nothing; but there again, no one had ever asked for details of my work before, so I doubted it would ever be mentioned.

CHAPTER THIRTY THREE
'Capers In Berlin'
West Berlin, Germany, 1982

No sooner had the news of Lt Linz's death been announced, his erstwhile friend, Kramer, also disappeared; which worried me, for Mister Dannet had recalled me to West Berlin.

"Panic not, my dear," he advised, upon my arrival, "we know exactly where to find him and the dead man's sister; but, only time will tell what their news will bring. If all has gone to plan, a game of political 'musical chairs' will soon take place behind the Wall."

Left with a mystified look and no explanation, I was given little time to respond.

"Now, our attention must turn to one Franz Rucker," he continued. "This gentleman may become a problem in the future; for his dreams of promotion to the East German leadership's inner circle could soon become a reality. As this is something we would like to prevent, I am giving you his file now; but, the timing of his removal depends on how other events unfold." Well, well, this was unusual, I'd never heard of anyone going on standby for a killing before.

Reading through the notes I was given, they told me that forty-five year old Franz Rucker was the new style politician, a handsome and polished individual who spoke well and was popular with the public. This meant his rise through the ranks was meteoric, the expectation being he would become General Secretary in the not too distant future. Needless to say, that didn't please Mister Dannet or his masters, who wanted the old guard to stagger on; better the devil you know, et cetera.

One detail was unusual, because of his trade portfolio; he was allowed to rent an apartment in the west of the city, where he stayed whilst on official business. This mostly concerned the export of their raw materials, in exchange for Western manufactured, luxury goods, for which there was huge pent up demand.

Ignoring the unnecessary details, it was obvious my only chance to eliminate Rucker would be when trade talks had him in West Berlin; so a detailed map of the area around his apartment block was needed. Supplied with this and suitably disguised, I spent many hours exploring this reasonable suburb, working on a scenario that might be possible.

All attempts to decipher Mister Dannet's previous ramblings merely gave me a series of blinding headaches; then all was revealed, though not by him. It was the television news that told me of a significant reshuffle within the East German government; both Voss and Baumann having been summarily dismissed, charged with discrediting the nation. This had Franz Rucker and an Erich Stoffel promoted to the inner circle; which wasn't exactly what Mister Dannet and friends wanted, but they didn't seem too unhappy about the result.

"Thank God, the pre-emptive strike nonsense has been debunked; Kramer and Miss Linz came up trumps in that regard, the video tape must have swung it for them," came on hearing the news. "Let us hope saner voices prevail from now on."

Or in plain English, our three East German agents had discovered the plans were actually for the yearly N.A.T.O. exercise, not an attack. The previously unconvinced Linz must have secretly filmed a planning meeting as proof of this, his video being delivered to the very top in East Berlin, instead of their nominal handlers.

Back at home, many months passed with no word of any problems; then Mister Dannet had me return to Berlin.

"As we expected, our Herr Rucker has begun to circulate nasty rumours about a friend of ours," he told me. "Behind the Wall, accusations of treachery are taken very seriously, so before this turns into a full scale witch hunt, you are to rid us of this man during his next visit here, which begins in a week's time. I trust you have read my notes?"

"Of course, though how am I going to eliminate this person and live to tell you?" this vexed person asked. "With the number of agents the other side has here; it won't take long for them to track me down."

"Timing may well be critical because of his planned, but short visit; but rest assured there will be an aircraft on standby at Tempelhof on the day of your choosing."

Not unexpectedly, my plan fell apart when he arrived at his apartment block, for there was a decorative young lady waiting to greet him; they went inside, while I spent the next two hours twiddling my thumbs. Thanks Mister Dannet, you didn't tell me about this, did you? On reappearing they headed for a red Beetle, her car presumably, and drove off with me frantically waving at a taxi.

After a 'follow that car' moment, both vehicles weaved their way through West Berlin's streets, eventually ending up at a parking place by the Grunewald. I alighted and paid my fare, then set off behind the loved up pair; who were in a world of their own, ambling alongside the River Havel in the evening light. Of course, there was no one else around when I suddenly had a gun barrel thrust in my back, a French voice muttering something about Monsieur Leon. Oh bugger, the past has reared its ugly head again, thought she, spinning round and shouting 'help!', while trying to wrestle the gun from my attacker.

This had Rucker run to my aid along with his lover, so he was quickly disarmed.

"The damn thing isn't even loaded," he exclaimed, on checking the weapon.

"No, but this one is," said a voice behind us, having me turn and face a big man pointing a sub machine gun at my head. "Okay you three, no talking, let's retrace our steps."

This we did, to be pushed into the back seat of a battered Ford estate car, which the smaller man drove.

"Where are we going?" demanded Rucker after a few minutes.

"You will be taken to Checkpoint Charlie, the walk home from there will do you good," was the reply.

"Don't be ridiculous, tomorrow morning I have to attend a vital trade meeting over here; there are important matters to discuss," he responded, having the big man's gun pointed at us again.

"Oh, come on. It's me you want, just drop the other two off somewhere," I pointed out, a suggestion which had the two up front muttering away in French.

We carried on through the fading light until stopped by a red light, where two other cars forced us into a cul-de-sac as soon as the lights changed to green. Before anyone could make a move, the side widows disintegrated and more guns appeared; oh Lord, this can't be happening, Mister Dannet's nightmare of Wild West antics in Berlin was coming true.

Roughly dragged from the Ford, the two from up front remonstrated with our masked kidnappers; a situation which quickly turned into a fight for control of the guns.

"Now's your chance, girl, get out and run like the wind," I whispered fiercely to Rucker's lady friend. "Don't worry about us, just go."

With a nod from her beau, she left us, sprinting away with her shoes off and skirt hitched up. Meanwhile, my target and I dived over to retrieve the weapons left in the car; but unfortunately, mine was the empty pistol. Once out in the open, Rucker foolishly tried to take control; waving the sub machine gun around and ordering the French pair to desist. A moment's relaxation from a masked figure had him at the wrong end of his own pistol, with the big man threatening to kill him if the rest didn't put their weapons down. This was ignored by the others, a burst of loud gunshots leaving two masked men on the ground moaning in pain; while Rucker staggered off with a leg wound. Rushing forward and scooping up an unattended pistol, I looked up to see the big man and my target now wrestling for control of the sub machine gun, their struggle compromising my aim. Taking a chance as this trial of strength continued, I fired, but the sudden stutter of automatic fire drowned out any noise from my two shots. This had both the big man and Rucker stagger apart and fall mortally wounded onto the tarmac. With no sign of the other Frenchman; both were confirmed dead before I left the scene, my departure hastened by the sound of approaching sirens.

CHAPTER THIRTY FOUR
'Discovery'
West Berlin, Germany, 1983

The hurried departure meant I have no idea who shot who in that final set to, but at least my objective was achieved; now for the final task. Slipping into Rucker's apartment block required the assistance of a resident, who took the concierge's attention as I entered and skedaddled up the stairs. Thankfully, searching his apartment for any incriminating evidence turned out to be easy, just as well for time was running out.

The sparsely furnished rooms and few personal belongings took just minutes to examine, leaving just one item for me to check; the wall mounted safe, unimaginatively located behind a large picture. Assuming it would be locked, imagine my surprise when the door swung open when I tentatively operated the handle. The contents consisted of one thin folder, where a quick scan at the pages within had my pulse racing; thoroughly convinced both East and West would kill for possession of this.

Stuffing the folder into my large handbag, I closed the safe and quietly left the apartment, making my way downstairs. A stroke of luck meant the concierge was busy helping an elderly resident into the lift, enabling me to leave the building unseen and have a car draw alongside me.

"Tempelhof, Madame?" asked the driver, through an open window.

Safely on board the aircraft and several thousand feet up in the sky, a copy of this folder was finally removed from my handbag and its contents read through.

Basically, it was an indictment of U.S. armaments manufacturers, who after making untold billions of dollars in defence contracts during the Second World War and virtually all conflicts since then; they were intent on maintaining that income stream, by actively prolonging the Cold War. Aided by certain military men and some of their own politicians, they were considering a plan to bribe Soviet and Chinese officials for their help; some even suggesting Cuba, Latin America and Africa could assist this cause.

Dear God, I thought, not content with helping to flatten entire countries and kill millions of combatants and civilians alike, they want the destruction and bloodshed to continue.

A second reading brought heightened alarm, for although the people mentioned were unknown to me, the detailed knowledge, facts and figures, et cetera, suggested the author had to be a senior executive in one of the company's involved; so what did this person hope to gain by revealing all this? Looking at it from every angle, there was never going to be any good coming from releasing this to the U.S. media.

Then another 'light bulb' moment: could this be a well researched, East German plan to have Washington take its eye off the current East/West tensions, by having to concentrate on the internal strife these revelations would cause? A clever idea and meticulous in its detail, but in my humble opinion, the expected result would never happen. Also, with Franz Rucker now dead, nobody would ever know what he intended to do with this information.

Disregarding all this, there was one major problem; once it became known I had found and taken this file, sooner or later someone would arrive in Biarritz to claim possession of it, by fair means or foul. So, for my own peace of mind, the original would remain in West Berlin; while this copy would stay with me no matter where I went.

My hope was that a certain Englishman would arrive on my doorstep to demand in his own unique style, that I hand it over. If those prayers were answered, he would soon learn that, because this was my one chance to reverse his hold over me; certain conditions must be met before anything changed hands. Once his agency honoured their commitment to the naturalisation and residence in the U.K. the file would be theirs; however, if the slightest hint of any funny business was detected during this process, they would find the prize had been given to other less friendly people.

On arrival back home, there was a letter telling me a substantial sum had been deposited in my Swiss account, it being the last communication for many weeks. I was starting to think my hopes were doomed; so a long delayed task of painting my front gate was begun; only to have my second day's toil ruined.

"Oh dear, I fear my presence will interrupt your good work," an English voice lamented, having me look up to see a smiling Connel Dannet stood by the newly coated ironwork, "may I come in, Marie?"

A nod had him dodge carefully past my handiwork; God forbid that any paint should sully the immaculate suit. While he made himself at home, I gave up and put the painting gear away, making coffee for us both.

"You have a lovely place here, Marie," he remarked, on receiving his steaming mug. "With the ocean next door and a balmy climate, it's got it all. I envy you."

"Thanks for the compliment, but you haven't come all the way here just to check out my domestic arrangements, so spit it out?"

"Quite so, my dear; firstly, despite Mister Rucker's messy death and its aftermath, it has achieved something which has been years in the making; we finally have a mole firmly embedded at the top table of East German government."

"Congratulations, I hope it makes you very happy," was my sarcastic comment, knowing full well he was talking about Herr Erich Stoffel.

"It does indeed; now secondly, the same impeccable source has informed us that you are in possession of a file, the contents of which are considered somewhat incendiary," he explained. "While many would like to exploit what this contains, we would prefer it to stay out of circulation for the time being. So, what price do we have to pay for you to hand it over?"

Well, as we all know, attempting blackmail is not the most sensible thing to do, but, my conditions were laid out; plus the penalty if should they fail to deliver.

"Ah, I have long wondered when that promise would be acted on," he replied knowingly. "Fear not, those on high have agreed to honour the whole retirement deal; but the start does require a sacrifice on your part. You will have to vacate this lovely home, journey to Paris and stay there for a few days; while remaining ready to move at a moment's notice. If this first episode meets with your approval, the process will begin in three days time."

That affirmed, he received a kiss on both cheeks, for a great weight was lifted from my shoulders; hooray, my precarious life was at an end, now what will a quieter future bring?

It was a wrench leaving Biarritz, but with my house and car already up for sale, I was transported away by an official car and driver to Paris; being left alone in a pokey one-bedroom apartment, surrounded by personal possessions. Well, the city beckoned, so a three day tour of my previous haunts took place; where I discovered the Karsch clothing empire had grown, having several swanky boutiques in the centre. There was something familiar at its impressive headquarters, Alain's pre-war limousine stood outside the glass front entrance, ready and waiting for the maestro. One treat was a cruise along the River Seine which ended at Pont d'lena. Never having done it before, I ascended the Eiffel Tower, slowly moving around the observation deck gazing at the magnificent views; wondering if it would be my last time here.
In need of cheering up, I had a night out; the delicious food and impromptu dancing at 'Lesbos' Greek restaurant had me return tired, sweaty and in need of a shower. Under the hot water and soapsuds, the vigorous washing suddenly had me go icy cold; for I felt a lump in my right breast.
After a sleepless night, I managed to arrange an immediate appointment with a private doctor, who after examining me, allayed my fears by saying the tumour may well be benign, but he would arrange further tests. I left somewhat relieved, arriving back at the apartment to find a note in its post box. This told me to be packed and ready first thing tomorrow morning, for a car and driver would arrive and take

me to my new home in England.

CHAPTER THIRTY FIVE
'A New life, Bad News'
Dorset, England, 1986

At last, I am settled in my small, eighteenth century cottage, located in a village called Dolhurst, which is a pretty little place, where my neighbours have made me welcome. However, getting to this stage had taken nearly a year, a lot of money and undue frustration, before it became the warm and cosy home of my dreams.

 The journey began in Paris, where my belongings and I were bundled on board a British registered vehicle, which then headed for Caen; a quiet journey for the driver was a man of few words, my questions left unanswered. We boarded the overnight ferry at Ouistreham, my voyage to Portsmouth spent sleeping in a warm, comfy lounge, far removed from the inclement weather outside. Disembarking in a queue of cars, our passage through Customs and Immigration was smoothed by some piece of paper that my driver handed over, though only when we drove off, did he hand over my new passport with a gruff 'look after it'. This last part of the journey was again carried out in near silence, as we weaved our way along a series of narrow roads to the destination. Entering the front door of my new home, had a familiar figure rise from his armchair.

"At last," cried Mister Dannet with a smile, "welcome to your new home, Marie, or Angelique, as I must call you now. Right, there is no time to lose, leave your luggage and come with me." With that we returned to the car and drove downhill to the seaside town of Swanscombe. There we visited a variety of offices, signed a blizzard of paperwork, all of which had me the registered, legal owner of the cottage, while contracted to pay for the use of its utilities. Not only that, a bank account had been set up, containing the monies from the villa and car sales in France. With all that complete we returned to Dolhurst and a welcome brandy.

"Now I think it's time you kept your side of the bargain, Angelique," Mister Dannet requested, after draining his glass. Opening my purse, I took out a key and handed it to him.

"The S-bahn station at Tempelhof: left luggage locker number eleven, your file is inside a red holdall."

"Thank you: now I must bid you farewell, for we shall not meet again," he replied, looking around one last time. "My masters have decided to put me out to grass, so the hope is both of us will have a long and happy retirement."

"As they say, time and tide waits for no man, Mister Dannet."

With that, I said goodbye and he left, driven off by my escort; leaving me feeling a bit deflated as their car disappeared from view, having to sit down and promptly fall asleep.

Next morning, there was time to properly examine my new home, which I judged to be in need of some updating, especially from the security point of view. It brought to mind something that Papa told me years back; remember this, my girl, he said, no one can stay unknown forever. No matter what, you always leave a trail, however insignificant, that others can follow. The best one can hope for is, to keep one step ahead; something that was impossible if like me, you are in a fixed location. So, as the nearest police station was some kilometres away, while patrol car visits were infrequent and random; it meant something had to be done.

From then on it was a non-stop period of improvements; I painted the inside, but had to pay a neighbour for the exterior to be done; while the discovery of dry rot meant the complete stairway had to be replaced, along with a few floorboards. Thankfully the roof timbers passed inspection, but it was still an expensive and time consuming performance, which combined with a financial wrangle, had me hopping mad. It was very hard to remain civil with a Swiss bank putting up every obstacle to prevent this customer from transferring their money to one in England. Nevertheless, with that eventually settled; the decision to change some of the furniture I had been left with, resulted in yet more delays; for every chosen item had a lead time of two months.

When frustrations boiled over, Nora, my next door neighbour, would advise me to relax, lie back, enjoy the sun and chill. This may have worked in her previous domicile, Singapore; but was impossible in a typical British winter, my first being the wettest I had ever experienced.

Come spring, I could be seen pottering around the garden; a small area that I was determined would rival the rest of the village's colourful displays in summer. Given guidance by Nora, my preparations and planting were completed in good time; the resulting flowers giving me much joy. This left a scrappy, miniscule patch of lawn, the source of much attention. Now, my treading on the rake wasn't planned, as its wooden handle flew up and hit my right breast so hard; I let out a blood-curdling scream. The commotion had Nora running to my aid, though her tea and sympathy weren't enough to dull the ache; but taking multiple painkillers meant I could sleep a little that night.

Next morning a taxi took me to the doctor in Swanscombe, who, after his examination, packed me off to the local hospital for a second opinion. There, various people in white coats conducted a series of tests, including x-rays; finishing by saying I should return in a few days to hear of the results.

"Are you prepared to hear some bad news, Ms Bergamont?" the senior consultant asked tentatively on my return visit, "for there is no way I can dress this diagnosis up."

Trembling slightly, I nodded.

"You have an aggressive cancer which is now spreading from the right breast to other parts of your body," he said quietly. "Unfortunately, my colleagues and I are in agreement that neither chemotherapy nor any medical procedures will do anything to arrest this development."

"In other words, you're saying my condition is terminal," my bland statement of fact had the brain go numb; barely hearing the medical jargon and his explanation of available drugs that might help, plus the various painkillers on offer. All I could hear was a voice inside screaming, 'after all the crap life has thrown at me, it has to end with this!'

CHAPTER THIRTY SIX
'DespairAnd The Lover'
Swanscombe, England, 1986

Still shaking, I stood outside the hospital wondering what to do; though an overpowering desire to drown my sorrows soon had me in the nearest pub, clutching a double brandy.

"Good God, you look like you've seen a ghost, what on earth's the matter, my dear," this soft voice made me jump in alarm. Turning to see a kindly face, my words came out in a rush, mixed in with tears.

"I think we better have you sat down," ordered the concerned gentleman, directing me to the upholstered chairs. "Now then, dry your eyes; take a deep breath and let's begin again."

After hearing my tale of woe, we sat quietly for a while; then he responded.

"All is not lost, you still have happy times ahead; so drink up, pamper that pretty face and let's go."

After repairing my ravaged make up, we left the pub and headed for the seafront, ambling along the promenade, each with our own thoughts.

"Oh Lord, I'm becoming forgetful," he suddenly said, "the name's Bob Watts, having a few days off at his favourite coastal resort. Going by your wonderful accent, I'm guessing you are French, yes?"

"Correct, my name is Angelique Bergamont, originally from Paris, but now a resident of Dolhurst."

Bob explained he worked for a German shipyard as an electronics technician, currently doing upgrades on their vessels. However, as the owners dictated their ships availability, his team ended up with odd days off between stays at ports all over Europe.

In turn, I told him of my retirement from British Government service, which as it was classified as 'secret', meant there was no way any details could be revealed.

"No problem," he replied knowingly. "Thanks to the Cold War, all of my sea time with the Royal Navy had the same restrictions."

We continued our walk until joining a mass of people all heading for the noise and commotion of a funfair.

"Right, you need cheering up, so no buts, we are going to try all the rides they have," said Bob, as he dragged me towards something which resembled a giant Catherine wheel. Well bizarrely, after being blinded by a myriad coloured lights while spun round and tossed every which way, I actually felt better.

"Right, I think we've exhausted their attractions, fancy something to eat?" Bob asked.

"That would be nice, once my stomach returns to its normal position," was my reply, looking forward to a light lunch in a nice restaurant. What I got was fish and chips in greasy paper, eaten while sat on the sea wall, surrounded by hungry gulls.

Meal consumed, we retraced our steps, carrying on till we reached an older apartment block, one designed with Mediterranean influences, having every balcony face the sea.

"While my dad was fishing off the beach, his young son watched this place being built," Bob recalled, "deciding there and then, one day I would buy a place here. It was the early nineteen-seventies before that momentous event took place and it remains mine. Would you like to see it?"

Having said yes, he escorted me to apartment 4B, where opening its front door, I was ushered inside. Um, the plain furnishings were in stark contrast to its beautiful hardwood floors, doors and window frames, my look having him explain that due to his work commitments, the apartment was rarely used; though he vowed that one day it would become his permanent home. In the meantime, much money and time was lavished on its maintenance; the woodwork being a major concern, for replacement timber was now virtually unobtainable.

"Well, this place must now be worth many times what you paid for it," I declared confidently, "you could always sell this and buy something that would make life easier."

"No, never, this is and always will be my home," he replied vehemently, "this is worth more than money to me!"

Afraid my comment had offended him, my arms went round his neck and I whispered.

"Be calm, I prefer a man who can display his emotions," a point which had me picked up and carried to a bedroom. There, discarded clothing was abandoned where it landed, as we fell onto the bed and made love. Lying there after it was over, he must have read my mind.

"Don't worry Angelique, every right thinking female needs to feel loved, if this is sincere; it's of no consequence whether the partner is younger or older than the lady in question."

"Thank you for that, now make love to me again," I purred, moving into his arms.

From then on, I made the most of every minute we spent together, random as those days were. When Bob hired a car, we spent most of our time exploring the rugged coast, well away from prying eyes; where I told him a censored version of my diving adventures. However as the years went by, I knew my condition was worsening, confirmed during my regular visits to the hospital; but it was one event in nineteen-eighty-nine that had me emotional and in floods of tears, Alain Karsch died after a short illness. In true theatrical style, the funeral was colourful and over the top; though he took his secrets to the grave.

Then, with Soviet Union support crumbling, the East German government fell into disarray; months of speculation and rumours ended with ordinary people pulling down the Berlin Wall. I rejoiced along with millions of others that the Cold War would soon be over; leaving the world to become an altogether better place.

CHAPTER THIRTY SEVEN
'The Last Goodbye'
Swanscombe, England, 1990

"My God, has it really been four years since we met?" I asked Bob, as we stood on his apartment's balcony, gazing out to sea. "Ah well, let's hope we have many more together."

 It was heartfelt, but I knew it was a lie, for my continual ache had grown worse during that time; the drugs now had no effect, while painkillers were needed more and more. During today's hospital visit I had been advised to prepare for the end; which was ironic as Bob was also due to fly back to Hamburg that very evening.

 Having forced myself to be bright and cheerful, there's no memory of what meal he cooked for us or what we talked about; but when it was time for goodbye, I remember clinging to him for a long while. The dread of it being our last time together, stayed with me long after the taxi took him away. I remained indoors to clean the apartment and then locked up, catching the last bus back to Dolhurst.

 The following morning and still tired after my fitful naps, it was coffee and painkillers for breakfast; while I contemplated doing some light gardening. That didn't go well, for barely an hour passed before pain and exhaustion had me back inside the cottage, desperate for more painkillers. Those taken I fell asleep, only awakening when Nora arrived with covered dish.

"I hope this salad comes with a morphine sauce," was my attempt at a joke, when it was revealed.

"That bad today, is it?" she queried, bringing me yet more painkillers and a glass of water. With lunch consumed and pills taken, we talked for a while; but the minute she left I fell sound asleep.

It was already dark when an unusual noise had me wide awake, the click of a light switch showing a black clad figure emerging from the kitchen.

"Stop right there," I cried, forcing myself to an upright position, "give me one reason why I shouldn't call the police right now."

"Alas, you have no mobile phone and they are too far away to make a difference; but this may," came as a sub machine gun was removed from the bag he carried and pointed at me. "Now, Mlle Marie Angelique Montagne, I know it's been a long time since we last met, but don't you recognise me?"

"No I don't, now for God's sake put that stupid thing away, your threat is meaningless. By the way, do you always come in via the back door when visiting people?" the question had me suddenly overcome with tiredness. "Oh never mind, so just who the hell are you and what do you want?"

There was a subdued stutter, unbelievable pain then darkness.

CHAPTER THIRTY EIGHT
'There Has Been A Murder'
Dolhurst, England. 1990

This lazy, hazy day of summer, saw just one small car travelling carefully along the narrow road to Dolhurst; a 'picture postcard' village and delightful place to live, situated high up on rolling hills, with enviable views of countryside and sea. Arriving in front of a small, but comfortable home, the car was parked, its blue uniformed driver alighting and making her way to the unlocked front door; she entered it only to discover the elderly resident inside had passed away. Now, anyone dying at that age would hardly warrant any official interest, but unfortunately the way of her passing was anything but normal, as other residents soon discovered. The arrival of several police cars and a pathology team inevitably had tongues wagging outside the cottage, a rumour rapidly spreading that their elderly friend had been killed!

Sadly, this was true, as Detective Inspector Ian Seymour soon found out on entering the property, for a woman's body lay awkwardly on the lounge carpet, her chest area a mass of blood, bone and human tissue.

"Oh good grief, what in God`s name happened here, John!" he breathed, staring at the macabre sight.

"What indeed," agreed the kneeling pathologist, still examining the victim alongside him, "Though I can tell you, this lady was obviously taken by surprise then shot multiple times at close range; look around the room, there are no signs of any struggle."

"So, this was no burglary gone wrong, but a premeditated act; any idea regarding the time of death?" Seymour inquired.

"Going by the state of her rigor mortis: somewhere between the hours of nine and midnight, last night. As usual, more precise details will be available after my post mortem. Can we remove the body now?"

The Inspector nodded distractedly, turning round to find his Sergeant approaching.

"Morning, Sir, nasty one this," he said brightly," the victim's name is Angelique Bergamont, possibly French, as the neighbours say she spoke with a noticeable accent. There's no sign of forced entry, so she either knew the killer or had left her front door unlocked. Inside, the cottage appeared untouched, with everything in its place. I have uniforms carrying out a detailed search of the property and garden, though I doubt we'll find any trace of the murder weapon."

"Maybe, we can but try," was his superior's reply," while you're at it get statements from all the other residents. Now, who found the body?"

"A Mrs Cawley, the District Nurse, she's outside with Joy, I mean, Constable Robbins, who is taking her statement."

The two policemen went outside and talked to the tearful nurse, who told them she couldn't understand why anyone would want to kill such a nice person. It would stain the reputation of this idyllic hamlet forever. Anyway, she continued, it was a totally stupid act, Ms Bergamont had already been diagnosed with breast cancer, which having spread to other parts of her body, meant she now had just weeks to live.

This morning's visit was for a check-up and discussion about her final arrangements.

This revelation stunned the policemen for a second or two, Seymour putting his hand up just as Detective Sergeant Morton made to speak.

"First things first, Terry, let's get back to the station and set up the incident room," he decided, "so we can examine all the evidence, whether it's from the victim's home or elsewhere. I already get the feeling this inquiry will present us with more than the usual tangled web of lies and distractions; what say you?" walking off towards his car before he received an answer. Morton waited until they drove off back to their base before replying.

"Is this because it looks like a gangland killing rather than murder, Sir," he queried.

"It's a possibility, plus I find it strange a foreigner would choose to live in such an out-of-the-way place, knowing she was suffering a terminal medical condition."

"Ah, you think Ms Bergamont was in hiding from someone who wanted revenge for some past wrong; there again, she might just have been the reclusive type?"

"Hardly likely," Seymour considered," however, first we have to assemble all the known facts."

CHAPTER THIRTY NINE
'The Investigation Begins'
Dorset, England, 1990

The next morning had Seymour shivering, pathology laboratories weren't his favourite places, all those white tiles, stainless steel and strange smells reminded him of childhood visits to an aunt, resident in what his school friends referred to as a 'lunatic asylum' or the 'looney bin'.

"Ah, there you are, Ian," the confident voice brought him back to the present, Doctor John Hawkes indicating for him to come closer to a body shrouded in white.

"Our victim, Angelique Bergamont, was a handsome female in her late sixties, five feet tall and of slim build; which means just one of six bullets I have removed from the body would have sufficed to kill her. All totally unnecessary especially as the lady was also suffering from terminal cancer."

"Yes, the District Nurse told us she had just weeks to live," interrupted Seymour, "oh, by the way, be advised, the name may not be correct."

"Right, thank you, to continue; the damage was done by a quick firing weapon, powder burns indicating it was used at close range; but curiously, there is no sign of any defensive wounds," the pathologist stated, exposing the victim's left thigh and waist. "However, these scars are from a previous bullet wound; she was lucky that time, it missed all the vital organs."

"Interesting, how old do you think they are?" asked

the now alert Inspector.

"Could be a wartime injury, but definitely sometime in the mid nineteen-forties; oh, by the way, your victim has had a child," he said, tapping an x-ray display screen.

Returning to his police station, Seymour went straight to their incident room and surveyed the scene; all the team were there, except their newly promoted, black Detective Constable; a formidable lady out to prove herself.

"Where is Jaynes?" he asked, having everyone point behind him, "Oh, well don't just stand there, Bobo, come in and sit down."

Explaining he still didn`t have a decent photograph of the victim, he relayed the pathology report, then asked what the team had found out so far.

"According to her naturalisation papers, her correct name is Marie Angelique Bergamont, previously a French citizen, who lived in Paris before moving over here," piped up Detective Constable Alec (Chalky) White, "I'm awaiting more details from the authorities over there."

"Now we know, I'd forgotten a lot of people don't like their first names, so never use them," said Seymour to no one in particular.

"Her bank shows our Marie was a fairly wealthy woman, making good returns on a variety of investments, Sir," stated Morton, "however, since the current account was set up five years ago, there have been no unusually large amounts withdrawn or credited to it. None of other paperwork taken from the house indicates the existence of separate accounts at different banks or building societies; but unfortunately, I doubt any foreign ones will co-operate with us on this matter.”

“Self sufficient, but the money must have originated from somewhere, find out where,” the Inspector’s order received a nod.

“The pathology report states bullets recovered from the victim were soft nosed .235inch calibre rounds, a single one being destructive enough to kill,” reported Bobo. “At present, only an Austrian based manufacturer is making weapons which use these; a sub-machine gun, developed for military use. As they have been bought for Special Forces use by various European countries, the odd one may have been smuggled into the U.K., but there is no record of any MOD procurement or official import,” handing over a photograph of the gun.

“Um, that complicates things,” commented Seymour, “our killer could have stolen and used this small weapon; which leaves us with a problem; it has been nearly forty-eight hours since the shooting, long enough for this person to destroy or export it.”

“Another point, sir,” added Bobo, “if our victim really was in hiding from a person, or persons unknown; could this have been a contract killing?”

“That would imply our retired lady was considered an important target,” he replied. “Unlikely but possible; which is why we urgently need every detail of her past life, from birth to her moving to England. Which reminds me; do the neighbour’s statements shed any light on the years she has lived in England?”

“The consensus of opinion has her as a likeable and generous person; Sir,” recalled ‘Chalky’ White, “popular because of her grace and charm, not forgetting an endearing accent. She would regularly talk with other residents, though all belatedly realised Ms Bergamont never mentioned anything about her personal or past life. Conversations were mainly about the present, future, her home and garden. Since moving there five years ago she has travelled around very little and then solely by bus or taxi; her only visitor from outside the area being the District Nurse. WPC Robbins is still at the crime scene, so we may learn more soon."

"Get her to talk to the residents again, along with the bus drivers on that route; while you can contact taxi firms in the area about our victim's trips. Right, let's get to it, there's a lot more we need to learn about this lady; meanwhile Bobo and I will find out how Ms Bergamont managed to obtain British citizenship without serving the normal ten year probation period."

CHAPTER FORTY
'Diplomacy Lessons, Warnings"
London, England, 1990

"Well, that warned us off, didn't it," remarked Seymour, as he and Bobo left the Foreign Office building after their initial enquiry was abruptly halted when an official trotted out the official line.

"In exceptional circumstances, a foreign national can be granted instant citizenship of this country."

"Yes, I am aware of this," the Inspector had replied politely. "But it would be of great help to our murder inquiry if we knew what exceptional circumstance applied to the victim, a sixty-nine year old French lady. Who as you know, didn't need a nationality change to live here permanently."

"I'm afraid Ms Bergamont's file is classified as secret, therefore no details can be released to any other agency. Furthermore, if you or your officers try other means to obtain information in the future, there will be penalties."

"Understood: I will convey your warning to my Superintendent, Goodbye and thank you for your time," he replied, pushing an annoyed Bobo towards the exit.

Out on the street, Seymour guided his constable towards a quirky looking coffee house, which they entered and ordered two lattes.

"Calm down Bobo, just be warned this town is full of self important jackasses."

"I'm alright now, Sir," she told him, "so, where do

we go from here?"

"Firstly, when those people mention secrecy and repercussions, I know it could mean big trouble for us in the future," he quietly warned her. "Secondly, there's a good chance we will be followed from now on, so keep your eyes peeled. Thirdly, we shall return to Dorset, there's nothing to gain by staying here."

So far the return journey had been a joy for Seymour, for today this infamous motorway wasn't its normal race track self; something which allowed him glimpses of colourful scenery they passed.

"Look in your mirror, Sir, I think we've been followed for some time now," revealed Bobo, ruining her superior's trip, "That blue Rover has maintained a three car distance behind us, come what may."

"Ah, yes I see him. Okay, a small diversion is called for; we will turn off at the next junction."

Sure enough, a few kilometres further on, as he indicated to enter the slip road, the blue car followed suit. They pulled off and headed for a roundabout, which covered in dense greenery, made their car invisible as it sped all the way round, to nearly tailgate the Rover as it turned off down a minor road. Dropping back a reasonable distance, both cars continued on until reaching a small town, where school run traffic was causing the usual chaos. Halted by a red light, the police officers lost sight of the other car; but unconcerned, Seymour continued along the main road through town till they reached countryside again.

"They're behind us again, Sir," reported Bobo eventually, to which he nodded, then asked for the quickest route back to the motorway. The cars stayed together until reaching the slip road, but the Rover was absent as they accelerated onto the highway.

"Well, I think that proves it," Seymour told Bobo. "We have definitely stirred the waters of their murky little pond. That little charade was for our benefit, signalling they will be watching us from now on. Inform the others to bear this in mind at all times and tell them it's no joke."

"I don't like being told what to do by those in London," muttered Superintendent Wallis, "though right now, they hold all the cards. Nevertheless Ian, you are to carry on with your inquiry, just be careful not to tread on their toes."

"Yes, Sir, understood," replied Seymour. "Oh, as the case hinges on what went on in France, can you arrange for one of my team to carry out investigations over there?"

"Consider it done," Wallis exclaimed. "By the way, this village, Dolhurst, I once overheard a damning rumour about the place. It was years ago, at some council shindig I had to attend, where one rather loud business type declared the only reason there had been building there, was to house retired security types who were under threat from the Russians. It was never confirmed, of course; but I am reliably informed some locals still swear it's true."

"Um, if it is one of those so-called 'secure locations', they picked a good spot. You never know, the truth is often stranger than fiction."

Back in the incident room, Seymour told the team of the aborted trip to London; then asked if there had been any progress.

"I'm afraid enquiries into her finances have come to halt, Sir, for most of the money was transferred over here from Switzerland," reported Chalky. "As usual, further details weren't forthcoming."

"You said most, what about the rest?"

"That's a strange one; it was a Government credit transfer from our Paris embassy, which judging by the amount, came from a house sale."

"Believable, but after the restrictions I've told you about, we'll have to leave at that," his superior ordered.

"Sir, STC, a taxi firm in Swanscombe, say our victim mostly used their services to and from her visits to the hospital, other times was to bring her home from the centre of town," Bobo read out.

"Um, not helpful: any news from the bus drivers?"

"Yes sir, WPC Robbins talked to those who drove the route, who said Ms Bergamont's trips were irregular, but always to or from the bus station in Swanscombe," noted Chalky. "They took notice of her because she was always nicely made up and smartly dressed. Oh, one more thing, on leaving the bus in town, she always headed for the sea front."

"Ah, that tells me she was going to meet someone special; I'll get the uniforms down there to ask around. Damn it, we need a better photograph than her death mask," Seymour complained. "Anything else to report, people?"

"We've heard back from Paris, sir," piped up Terry. "Our victim only stayed in the rented apartment for five days before moving over here; however, a further search revealed she had owned an apartment in another district from nineteen-forty-nine to nineteen-fifty-nine, before moving elsewhere."

"Meaning she must have been visible then," mused Seymour. "Is there anything else?"

"Yes Sir, curiously, according to the agent's

paperwork, Mlle Bergamont had only become a French citizen just days before buying that property.”
 “Oh Lord: more complications. Right, the time has come for one of you to be in France; any volunteers?” a request which elicited no response. “Come on, Terry, it’s on your CV, you speak the language.”
 “Alright, I’ll go, but, be warned, if my stay drags on, the family will kill me.”

CHAPTER FORTY ONE
'The French Connection Begins'
Paris, France, 1990

Terry Morton didn't know what to expect on arrival at Charles de Gaulle airport, but it definitely wasn't a very attractive brunette, who introduced herself as Officer Sylvie Marchand. Explaining that as the junior detective in the squad, naturally this assignment was given to her; the tone of voice suggesting it wasn't something she was looking forward to. The voice softened on discovering he spoke the language well, though she still hurried him to a multi storey car park to claim her car.

"I take you to your hotel first; then we have lunch before visiting Karsch," she explained, while carving her way through autoroute traffic at high speed, on the way into Paris. Her driving had him pressed back in his seat, the left foot searching for a brake pedal; but worse was to come once they were in the city. There, the chorus of horns objecting to her risky manoeuvres were answered with a shrug and much arm waving; his relief being visible when they eventually pulled up outside a small hotel.

His room contrasted with the rather dirty exterior, being a large, brightly decorated space with nice furnishings, he noted with pleasure. About to unpack his case, Sylvie dragged him away for another heart stopping ride through the manic traffic, ending up on a promenade alongside the River Seine. Presented with a bottle of beer, he watched as she tore her filled baguette in half, offering one end to him, adding a cheeky 'enjoy'. Actually he did, sat next to a beautiful woman who had plied him with food and drink, who wouldn't?

That pleasurable interlude ended with yet another frantic car ride, ending on arrival at an imposing, glass fronted building, its entrance door telling him this was Karsch Couturier. They were obviously expected, for a young man escorted them to the archive section, an area dedicated to the memory of Alain Karsch, founder and chief designer of the company. They wandered past examples of his most popular designs until coming to a room whose walls were covered with drawings of elegant young ladies wearing exquisite clothes. An elderly lady stood by as Morton looked around, zeroing in on the most prominent, for it pictured a thin, white haired man dressed in a blue suit and a solitary black glove. Though it wasn't that which had him transfixed, it was the eyes.

"That is the great man himself," the older lady informed him, "and this was his favourite mannequin, both drawn by Marco, our resident artist at the time."

"These were done for use on advertising posters and billboards," added Sylvie, as he looked at the fair haired woman pictured. Wearing a black creation, her matching high heeled shoes and thin gold necklace made sure the dress remained centre stage; though once again the eyes took his attention.

"Is that Mlle Marie Angelique Bergamont?" Morton asked.

"Yes, that is 'Miss Angel', as she was known," he was informed, "Our number one mannequin for a decade and much admired lady here in France, especially by her gentlemen friends." There followed a long conversation as she recounted the wonderful, crazy times, the success, failures and constant travel all over Western Europe. It ended by her telling him this particular portrait was done especially for Monsieur Karsch, shortly before Mlle Bergamont left the company.

"In that case, could I have some copies of this?" had the lady nod and rush off.

"Have you noticed their eyes?" he asked Sylvie, pointing at the pictures. "The artist has really captured that look of err, yes, a look of sadness about them; if I'm making any sense. Have you ever noticed this before?"

"Yes," she replied quietly, "on those who have suffered terrible ordeals or lost someone they loved deeply. They can laugh and smile, but the eyes don't light up."

"Here we are," broke their silent reflection, as Morton was given the pictures. "Such a pity she died in that car crash down south," the older lady recalled.

"Oh, when did this happen?" he asked in surprise, noticing Sylvie's frown.

"The spring of nineteen-sixty, she and her fiancé, Marc, died after their car left the road, somewhere inland of Nice."

Even after thanking everyone for their help, Sylvie still had an annoyed look as they left the building and returned to her car.

"Okay, what's got up your nose, Officer Marchand?" Morton asked.

"They're still peddling the same old myth," she replied scathingly. "Her reported death is still the subject of investigation. It is on record that after the accident, a policewoman was sent to Defarge's home, where a lady she recognised as Mlle Bergamont was told of what happened. However, she wasn't there when identification of the body was required, nor was ever seen again."

"Well, this might help, I reckon these two faces are one and the same person, don't you?" he replied, showing the mortuary photograph to Sylvie, who nodded. "Right, I need to get these drawings to my boss double quick; then it's back to my hotel, where I can spend all evening wondering what 'Miss Angel' has been doing for the last thirty years."

"Or, you can take me out for dinner instead," she ventured.

"You do realise I am a married man with two children."

"All the better, for I will be safe from wandering hands or worse," the laughing Sylvie countered. "Plus, our conversation won't have to mention anything about police work."

Despite his imaginings, Sylvie didn't arrive in sky high heels, a plunging neckline or short skirt, but wore a rather stylish dress. Taking him to a restaurant near the river, they had a very pleasant evening together, enjoying a delicious, but expensive meal, while discovering what each other's life outside of work consisted of. And no, there wasn't a word said about their present careers.

Next morning, a smiling Sylvie arrived, but instead of driving off, they went to a nearby cafe.

"Okay, give me a clue, Sylvie, where do we start looking?" Morton asked, nursing his coffee. "Mlle Bergamont's early life is a complete blank; while her disappearance in nineteen-sixty is that far back; most people will have forgotten what happened by now."

CHAPTER FORTY TWO
'Details, We Need More Details'
Swanscombe, England, 1990

Satisfied that every beat officer now had a drawing of their victim, Seymour hoped they would soon discover who she visited; praying it would add to their knowledge of her past.

 As he reminded Chalky and Bobo, so far, they knew Ms Bergamont was a Caucasian, born in nineteen-twenty-one, but not where or in which country. The details in her passport are false, but why would she have to apply for citizenship if already French? Similarly, her upbringing and early life are unknown, up until her appearance in Italy. According to records in Paris, her application was submitted in Rome; an action quickly rubber stamped. No reason was given for this, though it suggests she did something important for France during the Second World War; which could be connected to that bullet wound she received.

 The next period of our victim's life is well documented, though photographic evidence proves she wasn't present in that car crash. Then, yet again there is a twenty-five year blank until she appears in Dolhurst.

 "Now, pre-war days will be a major problem," Seymour admitted, "but, I don't believe anyone so well known in the 'sixties could suddenly become invisible, the modern world doesn't work like that."

 "Could our victim have been born in Belgium?"

asked Chalky, "half the population have French as their first language, while a lot of the Flemish speakers are also fluent."

"That's a good call, but it will take an age to find the details we need," was his answer, "but, I will pass it on to Terry. Now, is there any more news?"

"We have just been handed two items found in the cottage by Forensics, one file and whatever this is," reported Bobo. "They report the only fingerprints on them were our victim's."

After reading the contents of the file, Seymour grunted, having noticed it was a copy.

"As the Cold War is now history, it doesn't matter whether this indictment is true or false," he told the team. "However, if our friends in the security services discover we have this, you don't need me to repeat what will happen. We will hide it away until it is needed."

"This thing looks like some kind of basic map or chart," stated Chalky, after examining the yellowed paper. "Trouble is there's none of the usual markings you expect and God knows what those red blobs and black dots represent." His superior looked, noting the ragged bottom line and one hundred and eighty degree arc drawn on it; racking his brain for what all this was meant to tell the viewer. Giving up on that, he asked if any other information had been unearthed.

"One thing, Sir," called WPC Robbins, entering the incident room. "The postman in Dolhurst told me Ms Bergamont received letters written by the same hand from all over the continent, every one of them a port city. This latest one is from Hamburg."

Given the airmail envelope, a smiling Seymour returned to his office, convinced it would give his inquiry the boost it needed.

"Excuse me, Sir, there's one more thing," interrupted Robbins. "There's something strange about the residents of Dolhurst, I met two men equipped with binoculars, who claimed to be bird watching; but when told of the yellowhammers, they appeared mystified, even though some were flitting about in a nearby field."

"Don't worry, Joy, you've made my day, as well as confirming a rumour."

Opening the letter and reading its contents left him with one thought; they had just two weeks find out where this gentleman, Ms Bergamont's lover going by what was written, lived in Swanscombe.

Actually, it was two days later when a Constable on beat duty reported two residents of the seafront promenade had recognised the subject of the drawing. Both were certain she went to Selangor House, a block of twenty four apartments.

"Right Bobo, with me, we're going to the seaside," ordered Seymour, "if I talk nicely to the council, they should tell us who this 'Bob' is."

"You mean William, surname unknown, a marine electronics technician."

"Quite, are you always pedantic about these matters, Bobo?" queried her superior. "If so, you can drive," coming as she received the ignition keys.

"Told you, treat a civil servant with some respect and they will respond," Seymour told Bobo as they left the council building, heading for the sea front.

"You mean that young man, the one who ogled my bosom from the minute we entered the office," she spat back.

"Why get upset, shouldn't you actually be proud of

your natural assets?" he countered. "I say this because going by what people have recalled, it points to our victim being very active sexually during her life. Now, I'm not accusing her of being a whore or prostitute; rather, that fact could mean more than one person will remember her and reveal important information to us. Never forget, most inquiries will need every avenue explored, so you must maintain an open mind."

There was no reply as they headed for Selangor House to locate the apartment belonging to William James Watts, though Bobo was appreciative of the building's design. Satisfied, they returned to the station, after telling the officer on that beat to keep an eye open for the occupant of apartment 4B.

CHAPTER FORTY THREE
'French Fancies Come Good'
Paris, France, 1990

"I think we should begin from nineteen-sixty on, because the pre-war records could have been lost or destroyed," Sylvie told Morton. "The best thing is to circulate that drawing in places which your victim would have preferred."

"How do we divine those?" he replied.

"Well, being the petite sort, I'm guessing she would prefer somewhere warm," was his answer. "Down south, but forget the Mediterranean coast; that's for the rich and famous, not someone intent on hiding away. My choice is the south west and Atlantic coast."

"Okay, let's go for that, if your superiors are in agreement."

Having been given permission, by the time a week had passed they were inundated with reports of sightings; which had Officer Marchand allowed to accompany Morton to Bayonne, where they would be based. After sorting through the mass of paperwork, it soon became clear a lady calling herself Juliana was either the real Mlle Bergamont, or her double. Also, the majority of sightings occurred along the Atlantic coastal region, but never in one specific place.

"It's time to confer with the mayor of Biarritz," Sylvie decided, when they had everything in order of importance.

"Why there?" queried Morton.

"Because, discounting the tourist trade, it has a large resident population."

Sylvie was all smiles on returning from the meeting, reporting the mayor had helped her to discover a property that had been owned by one Juliana Legrand, from nineteen-fifty six until nineteen-eighty-four.

"It's a lovely place right on the coast, but half hidden by trees; ideal for a hideaway," Sylvie enthused. "Neighbours told me the owner was a busy single lady who lived there alone; though oddly, she had few visitors, but was always going away on business trips. The best thing, all of them said the drawing was of her, a fashionable lady who knew good design; some even thought she might be a journalist working for some women's magazine."

"So, this Juliana was really Mlle Bergamont, who hid herself away after her fiancé died," Morton mused. "The question is, why the need to hide and adopt an alias?"

"I can't answer that, but a curiosity was found regarding the house," Sylvie told him. "When it came up for sale, prospective buyers had to negotiate with a law firm based in Paris. My enquiry revealed they do a lot of work for the British Embassy."

"Keep that to yourself: our security services have made it clear, they don't want us meddling in their affairs," he warned. "Now, should we investigate Marc Defarge?"

"No need, he was the ultimate self publicist of a businessman, plus several books have been written about his wartime heroics. Though, none will mention his drug addiction."

"Oh Lord, it's becoming obvious the reason for our victim's sudden change goes back to events during the war or its aftermath," Morton sighed. "It's a long shot, but maybe she was involved with her killer then."

"Why not before the war," argued Sylvie, "people grew up earlier in those days; aged eighteen she could already have a long criminal past. However, I think she was well schooled, you can't suddenly have the poise, walk and style of a mannequin, yet according to the Karsch employees your victim did."

"So you agree with me, sometime between nineteen-thirty-nine and 'forty-nine was the start of all this; remember, someone shot and wounded her during that time, that person could be our killer."

"Yes, plus I'm certain Mlle Bergamont was born and brought up in Belgium, but how she ended up in Italy is anyone's guess," admitted Sylvie.

"I think you're right, same language, et cetera; so how do we persuade the Belgian authorities to work with us?"

"Well, they will need a lot more information than we have right now; for a start, her real name and place of birth would help," Sylvie reminded him.

"Okay, one mad idea, would it help to ask the newspapers in Rome to publish that drawing, asking if anyone remembers seeing her there during the immediate post war years?"

"I think you have to try that in every country she visited, because we have learnt very little about her private life, friends or lovers; one of those could lead us to, or is the killer. Remember, your inquiry is running out of time and options, we need some progress or otherwise this will become another cold case," she concluded.

CHAPTER FORTY FOUR
'More Details Emerge'
Swanscombe, England, 1990

"William James Watts?" asked Seymour showing his warrant card to the harassed looking man who opened the front door of apartment 4B, Selangor House. Watts nodded, so he and Jaynes explained why they were there.

"Oh Christ, that bloody cancer," was the emotional response, having the police officers escort him to the lounge and sit him down.

"No sir, I'm afraid not, she died of gunshot wounds received ten days ago, so her death is now subject to a murder inquiry," a statement which had him slump down, almost in tears.

"What! For God's sake, why would anyone kill a dying woman?"

"That is what we are trying to find out," Seymour explained gently. "Now, if you are feeling up to it, we have some questions." After handing back that last letter with an apology, Watts was asked, if during their relationship had Ms Bergamont ever mentioned anything about her past life.

Well, he recalled, she let slip about being born in Belgium, but not where. Also, when talking of past relationships, she told him her first love, Andre, was killed by the Nazis in nineteen-forty-three; while a lot later in nineteen-sixty her fiancé, Marc, died in a car crash. Despite other lovers coming and going, she thought herself fated to never have a long term relationship. She told him many stories about her time in the fashion world, but never mentioned the following years; except to say that her work for the British was classified as 'secret' and therefore never spoken about.

"Now a lot of my time spent in the Royal Navy was treated as 'top secret', so I can guess what she was doing."

"What might that be?" asked an intrigued Bobo.

"Oh come on, Angelique could speak fluent English, German as well as French and she was active during the Cold War; it was obviously intelligence gathering of some sort," Watts stated.

"One more question, Mister Watts, did she ever mention having a child?" asked Seymour, receiving a shocked look and vigorous shaking of the head. "Right, that's all for now, but if you remember anything more, however trivial, please phone us at this number."

Returning to the incident room, Seymour looked at their board, photographs and notes written on it, before turning to the team.

"Right, it's a fact that Ms Bergamont had a baby, but with no mention of this post war, I'm guessing her wartime lover, Andre, was the father. Now, even in those times, having a child out of wedlock was frowned on, so was it given away, adopted or killed? We need to find out because, if this individual is still alive, it's possible he or she could be our killer."

"This has just come in from Terry, Sir," Chalky. "Emilio Ligari, an Italian art restorer, had contacted him, to say he met Marie in nineteen-forty-six, on a beach north of Naples. He judged her educated, but troubled, for both were destitute at the time, living off what the land and sea gave them. So soon after the war, meant their respective pasts were never mentioned; but both were determined to succeed in this new era. He learnt this after they journeyed to Rome, where her passable Italian was ignored, for he encouraged Marie to learn English. To everyone's delight she reached fluency remarkably quickly, the tutor finding a job to suit her poise and natural style. Working in a fashionable shop, had her modelling clothes for prospective buyers; something that eventually led her to Paris."

"I gather they were lovers, going by his effusive offering," Seymour observed drily. "Did he mention anything pertinent to our inquiry?"

"Yes, Sir, Marie let slip that she had been treated for a gunshot wound at a charity hospital in Naples, after Mister Linari had pointed out her still livid scars. Subsequent enquiries by the Italian police, revealed a report from the end of World War Two stating, a railway worker inspecting one recently arrived goods train from Rome had found her lying comatose in an empty wagon. After her treatment, the hospital confirmed that she worked there for a year without pay."

"Oh Lord, more questions than answers; though Marie could have been in France or Italy at the time, it proves her shooting had nothing to do with any military action," mused Seymour. "That leaves us with crime or revenge as a motive."

"With her knowledge of German, Marie would have been an ideal candidate for the Resistance movement," suggested Chalky. "Maybe this Andre was already involved and persuaded her to join, which led to their child, his death and eventually the shooting."

"Well, that's something we can definitely check out,
I'm sure Officer Marchand will show us how," was
the answer.

CHAPTER FORTY FIVE
'The Victim's Life Becomes Clearer'
Paris, France, 1990

"Good news, Sylvie?" asked Morton, after she returned from consulting the wartime records of the Resistance movement.

"Well, I can tell you that during the occupation Andre Bergamont and Marie Montagne were part of a group operating in the Ardennes region of eastern France," answered his question. "But, both reportedly died in nineteen-forty-three when they were betrayed to the Nazis. If this couple are who we suspect; it's possible Marie could have escaped death and fled, using the Bergamont surname from then on, remember, she had no papers when in Italy."

"At last, this will move our inquiry along," cried Morton, blowing Sylvie a kiss. "We can give the Belgians her correct name, Marie Angelique Montagne, and her date of birth, April the ninth, nineteen-twenty one in, aw hell, I don't know, Ostend maybe?"

"Why there?" queried Sylvie.

"Well, apart from Brussels, it's the only other place I've been to in Belgium; you know the ferry port," he confessed.

"Okay, we have to start somewhere, I suppose," she reluctantly agreed. "If they are willing to co-operate with us, the details will be sent."

"Well, after a day spent rereading the reported sightings of our victim on the Atlantic coast, I discovered one solitary fact, not that it helps our inquiry in any way; our Marie was an avid scuba diver for many years."

"Don't discount it, that hobby might have led to something we can use."

"Oh, one thing I picked up from Yves Montard, who ran the dive school Mlle Bergamont attended in the 'sixties," recalled Morton. "He remembers being told she was a freelance fashion journalist, doing articles for several women's magazines."

"With her previous career as a mannequin, plus her frequent absences from home, that rings true. However, it could be a cover for something completely different."

"Why are you so suspicious?" he asked.

"Because I find it strange she should suddenly change careers during those missing twenty five years, for she retired as a British intelligence operative; those people are chosen because of their background or similar experience in that work."

"Maybe, but I think it's worth checking out, Juliana Legrand could be her nom de plume," Morton insisted.

First thing the next morning Morton received a visit from their postman, being presented with a large package.

"Oh Lord, look at this lot," cried Morton, after opening this special delivery from Germany. "It's reported sightings of our victim and going by the number of them, she must have spent some time there."

"Well, that mad idea of yours worked," said Sylvie in admiration, "Enjoy your day, I'm off to check if Mlle Bergamont really was a fashion journalist."

His reply was inaudible as a space was cleared for the mass of paperwork, but he soon settled down to the task. Eight hours and many cups of coffee later, he had ascertained that Marie had spent most of her time in the north of West Germany and more worryingly, West Berlin.

"This isn't looking good, Sylvie," Morton remarked when she returned to the office. "If these sightings are correct, from nineteen-seventy-one until 'eighty-three our Marie spent a lot of time in Berlin; which ties in with Mister Watts view that she was involved in intelligence work for our security services."
"Oh great, we will hit a blank wall trying to investigate further," she replied, thinking hard. "Unless: those sightings can be connected to some event that happened around the same time. By the way, what was it that made Mlle Bergamont visible there?"
"This might explain it," Morton said, pointing at one note. "It reports our victim was easily recognisable because of her small stature and the ability to make a humble tee shirt and jeans look like high fashion; despite any changes to her hair colour or make up."
"Well, it proves the Cold War made everyone more observant than normal in that city."
"No doubt, now to other matters, what did you learn from France's magazine world, were the rumours true?" Morton asked.
"Yes: and you were right, the articles were attributed to a Juliana Legrand," Sylvie confirmed, "She supplied fashion news to three women's magazines from nineteen-sixty until 'seventy one. Mind you, the combined salary wouldn't have been enough to support her home, car and travel; so she must have

had savings from her mannequin days. Anyway, all the employers say they were pleased with her contributions, but were surprised when she decided to retire. The reason for finishing was the time honoured 'to pursue other interests'."

"Or as we surmise, a more lucrative form of employment," he retorted.

"Which brings us back to my previous question; apart from experience with the Resistance, what qualification did she have for intelligence work?" Sylvie asked. "I'm sorry, but we are missing something here; let's hope Ostend can provide some answers."

CHAPTER FORTY SIX
'Details ,Yes, Motive, No'
Swanscombe, England, 1990

"Oh, my God, look at this, Sir," Chalky called. "The news from Belgium: records show that a Marie Angelique Montagne was born on the correct date, in an Ostend hospital. Mother-Juliana Legrand, a seamstress, father- Leon Montagne, occupation unknown."

Their expenses were paid for in cash a fortnight later, Chalky continued, the family leaving for an unknown destination. Further enquiries revealed they settled in the village of Berhout, near the country's southern border. Just before the Second World War began, they moved again, south to Mistou in the Ardennes region of France and were never heard of again.

"Now listen to this, Belgian police searched through their records, to find the name Leon Montagne was renowned in their criminal circles for being a 'hit man'," Chalky read out. "Though suspected of carrying out many killings, this elusive figure was never formerly accused nor charged, because the police couldn't find any evidence that linked him to those crimes."

"Oh, that has me thinking some crazy thoughts," Seymour revealed. "Could this all boil down to, like father, like daughter? Think hard before dismissing it, for it could explain some of the unusual aspects of this inquiry."

"A trained killer and fashion model, well anything's

possible I suppose," added Bobo. "Our problem will be proving it."

"Ah, could all of this started with our Marie joining the Resistance?" suggested Chalky. "Having a crack shot with rifle and pistol with them was definitely a bonus. I am willing to bet that the SOE soon found out about that fact, recording it for future use."

"Okay, let's not get carried away, like Bobo said, we need proof," Seymour reminded them. "I think Officer Marchand is on the right track; connecting sightings of Marie to an unexplained killing could be the way forward."

Seymour returned to his office, sitting there going through what they had discovered and whether any of it related to the victim's killer and their motive. An hour later he considered their enquiries should focus on events from nineteen-forty to forty-five, now convinced the reason for Marie's odd behaviour and eventual demise began during that time. The only niggling doubt was, why had it taken forty-five years before the killer managed to confront his victim? No matter, they had to start somewhere, so he contacted Morton and told him to find out everything about this Mistou and its inhabitants.

Also, he considered their stalled investigation of Marie's child; a complete lack of information meant there was no official way to confirm where the baby was born, so, was there another way? Convinced the child would have been adopted, therefore a record of this must exist somewhere; the Inspector added the task of finding out where, to Morton's list.

However, already receiving complaints from his Sergeant's wife about the length of time her husband had been in France, Seymour prepared himself for more when she heard of the latest demands; but who else could he send there? Chalky didn't know a word of French, while Bobo had a reasonable knowledge, but her lack of experience might hinder rather than help things along. However, in spite of his misgivings and unwilling to be the subject of a family breakdown, he decided Bobo would have to take Morton's place in Paris; whilst praying that she and Officer Marchand would get on.

Much to his surprise, Bobo was enthusiastic about having this chance to broaden her horizons, while she secretly hoped this would also help the chances of promotion.

CHAPTER FORTY SEVEN
'A Change, a Revelation, Then Another'
Paris, France, 1990

On arrival at Charles de Gaulle airport, Bobo was stunned that her new colleague was a very attractive young lady, who Morton introduced as Sylvie.

"Don't you dare tell anyone, especially my wife," he pleaded, "she thinks, Officer Marchand, is a man. If she found out I had been cavorting around France with a beautiful woman, my life won't be worth living." His goodbyes were accompanied with laughter as he disappeared into the airport departure lounge; the ladies heading off to the car park, Bobo eager to see Paris for the first time.

Surprisingly, her new friend's driving style was ignored; their quick tour of all the sights taking equal amounts of concentration and delight, before they stopped for Sylvie's favourite lunch, a beer and shared baguette.

With the short break over it was back to work, having Bobo looking for events that corresponded with sightings of Marie. By the evening it was apparent Sylvie's idea could be correct, for between nineteen-seventy-one to 'eighty- three, she found that three unexplained deaths and a fatal traffic accident had occurred at the same time there were sightings of Marie. The only anomaly was Hamburg, where there had been sightings of her kidnap by bank robbers, but no report of any unexplained death, which was odd.

However, that one Russian engineer, two East German spies and one of their politicians constituted victims of homicides; it convinced Bobo all were eliminated at the behest of British Intelligence, with Marie as their chosen implement.

While she relayed her findings back to Seymour, enquiries about wartime adoptions weren't going well, Sylvie being asked for the mother's exact location, sex and age of the child, before any investigation would begin. She couldn't answer their questions nor give an educated guess, though convinced the birth would have occurred in nineteen-forty-four; so her thoughts turned to this place, Mistou. Unable to find it on any map, she made an appointment with the Ardennes local authority to find out more, curious why it had been omitted.

Both she and Bobo found out the next day, when an official guided them to what had been the village square. This, the only unobstructed area, contained a single marble slab detailing all those who died when the place was destroyed in nineteen-forty-three; while the surrounding mounds of stones and bleached wood bore silent witness to the destruction. They learnt all bar three of the residents perished during this barbarous act of retribution.

"Christ, they shot one hundred and twenty nine people?" queried the horrified Bobo.

"No, every man, woman and child were locked in a barn, then burnt to death," replied Sylvie quietly. "It was done in revenge for the shooting of an S.S. officer."

"Oh my God, oh my God," muttered Bobo repeatedly, going quiet on noticing there was no mention of Marie or her parents; only to remember she and Andre supposedly died prior to this massacre.

"Monsieur Montagne and his wife died while being held prisoner by the Wehrmacht, two weeks before the village was destroyed," the official answering her unasked question.

Back at his office, he told them they weren't the first to enquire about the Belgian man and his wife; according to their records the first was, Pierre Lequet, who in nineteen-sixty-four, had requested the address of their daughter. After being informed of her death, this man left; though later on one of the clerks remembered something important. Searching out a wartime document, it confirmed Monsieur Lequet and two other members of the Resistance had been arrested, put on trial and were executed in nineteen-forty-three. The police were informed of this, but they heard no more.
 The second occasion was well remembered, for it was he who attended to this very smart lady; a lawyer, who needed their details to sort out an inheritance.

"Do we assume it was Marie who shot the S.S. officer," asked Bobo as they drove back to Paris. "It makes sense to me, with her parents and lover all killed by the Nazis, revenge must have been on her mind."
 "Very likely, also I think she was the lawyer, seeking to sort out her own inheritance," Sylvie replied. "For many years a lot of European people have put their ill gotten gains in Swiss banks and still do, it's not illegal."
 "That would tie in with what we already know about Marie's finances. Now, what about this Pierre Lequet, do we place him on our list of suspects?"

"Definitely, I detect the smell of a Nazi collaborator," declared Sylvie. "Did you notice there were sixteen members of the Lequet family on that memorial; so did he know Marie had killed the S.S. Officer and has been looking for her ever since, to avenge his family's deaths?"

"It's a long time to hold a grudge," commented Bobo. "But surely after the liberation, evidence of his collaboration would become known, having him a wanted man?"

"Correct, which would have left him with just two options, flee the country, or join the Foreign Legion. In post war Europe, the first would be impossible without ample money to survive on; leaving the second as an obvious choice. Once recruited, your past no longer exists, plus, finishing your service with an honourable discharge, allows you to walk away as a new person."

"Leaving him free to continue his search unhindered," added Bobo. "Okay, if we assume that's true, how can we prove your theory, I don't see the Legion letting a foreign police force poke about in their archives?"

"You're right, but once a civilian, he must have had a passport and some kind of work to finance that search for Marie, so we will start there," concluded Sylvie.

CHAPTER FORTY EIGHT
'Suspects, Motive, But Problems'
Swanscombe, England, 1990

At last, Seymour could report to his Superintendent that they had two possible suspects for the murder of Ms Bergamont, despite both being virtually unknown.

"Well done, I agree with you, Ian, this Pierre Lequet and your victim's child have motive," Wallis agreed. "Now, what have we learnt about these two individuals?"

His superior didn't look too pleased when told tracing Marie's child had proved virtually impossible, because at the time of birth, she could have been anywhere between Ardennes and Naples; so, actual date of birth and gender remain unknown.

In nineteen-forty-three, nearly all of the Lequet family were resident in Mistou at the time of the massacre except, Pierre, a member of the Resistance, who was later reportedly arrested, tried and executed by the Nazis. This was proven false when France was liberated, for he became a wanted man, charged with being a collaborator; Officer Marchand had seen the document, which is marked 'unresolved'. He disappeared completely until 'sixty three, when issued with a passport in Marseille. D.C. Jaynes and Officer Marchand have since discovered he served with the Foreign Legion from 'forty-five to 'sixty, when he suffered a mental breakdown. Given an honourable discharge, his next three years were spent in a psychiatric hospital, until judged to have fully recovered and returned to civilian life: From then till retirement in nineteen-eighty-five he was a dockland security supervisor. According to his staff he was obsessed with 'Miss Angel' as our victim was known during her mannequin days. Jaynes was convinced this is because he wanted to exact revenge, holding her responsible for the deaths of his family.

"My problems now are: who revealed where Ms Bergamont lived and where is Lequet now?" explained Seymour. "Also, why are those in London so jittery about this case, it's almost as if they are involved somehow."

"With their warning, plus what you have discovered, I would say that's a given," Wallis agreed, "Though, why show their hand so early, that's almost an admission of involvement in this killing; it makes me wonder who they coerced into abetting the murderer?"

"Perhaps London expected us to quickly overstep the mark, so they could close down the inquiry or have it transferred to Scotland Yard, where lack of evidence would soon have it a cold case."

"You have a poor opinion of our masters, Ian," noted Wallis.

"I have no trust in politicians or security types, Sir, especially those who bend the law to suit their own agendas. As we were taught when children, nobody is above the law."

"Are you inferring that London thought your victim's affair might wreck the security of their 'safe area', so Lequet was let loose to rid them of an embarrassment?" he asked.

"That is exactly what I think, for it would be impossible for him to learn of the move to England."

he stated. "Although they must have miscalculated, surely London would have preferred the murder be carried out in Swanscombe; thereby ensuring newspaper reports came from there and nowhere else. I can't see much interest being taken in one foreigner found guilty of killing another in that town."

"That's a big assumption, though I take it you are certain that Lequet will be in custody soon?" Wallis asked. "So everything can return to normal, leaving Dolhurst to remain the forgotten village. In an ideal world maybe, but can you deliver, Ian?"

"That is up to London, Sir, if they want everything wrapped up nice and neat; we should soon have information pinpointing his location, allowing us to arrest this man. If that doesn't happen, we are looking at some other agenda being played out; trouble is, I have no idea what that might be."

"As before, Ian, proceed with caution," Wallis concluded.

CHAPTER FORTY NINE
'Final Pieces Of The Puzzle'
Paris, France, 1990

After studying all the reported sightings of Marie in France and Italy, Bobo felt there was something missing.

"Were the drawings distributed in the east of the country, Sylvie?" she asked. "I know it's a long shot, but the most direct way from Ardennes to the border with Italy lies there. Despite the fact it was nearly forty-five years ago in wartime, someone, somewhere along that route might remember our victim."

"Come to think of it, no, Trevor and I were concentrating on the west coast in the 'fifties and 'sixties then," was her answer. "Well, we are truly stuck regarding Marie's child, so consider it done. One thing in our favour, childbirth in adversity is normally well remembered by those involved."

"Could we have a police artist draw a younger version of Marie, it might help jog memories?" suggested Bobo, who received a nod.

It was four days before they received any replies, where all but one were rejected as false memories; this last from a Claudette Jeans sounded promising. She claimed to be the daughter of a midwife, who in nineteen-forty-four assisted at the home birth of a baby boy named Andre. The mother, known only as Marie, wasn't a local, but lived with an Italian lady, Celeste Mandini, who had taken her in several months before. The child departed several weeks later, Celeste and Madame Jeans having arranged with the Mother Superior at Saint Cecilia's to have the baby adopted.

Days after the war ended, Marie disappeared, while Celeste returned to Italy after her house was sold; neither of them seen again.

"Time to visit Languedoc," cried Sylvie. "Also to investigate any unexplained killings in the south after the war ended. I have the feeling Marie's career as a hired killer began then."

"You think the wartime killings were used to blackmail Marie by those in our intelligence service?"

"Later on maybe, but not at the start, collusion between the former Resistance and the Gaullists would be more likely; but proving that would be nigh on impossible," Sylvie concluded.

Bobo reported back to Seymour about the birth of Marie's child and its subsequent adoption, a delicate negotiation at St Cecilia's nunnery that she left to her French colleague. Offering an afternoon of explanations and expectations, Sylvie learnt that, Andre Montagne, was adopted by a British couple, a Mr and Mrs Macintyre. There was no explanation of how their child was transported to Berne, Switzerland, where Mister Macintyre served as a diplomat; however, the Mother Superior was told all had gone well.

As for any unexplained deaths, they learnt of just one, in nineteen-forty-five, at Menton; though going by the paperwork, none of those involved with the police inquiry were particularly worried about the death of a Nazi collaborator, for the case remained unsolved. The only telling clue for Bobo and Sylvie;

was that the murderer must have also been shot and wounded, for there were two sets of bloodstains at the crime scene, with more on the apartment's balcony.

"I do believe we have found the reason for Marie's scars and her escape to Italy," exclaimed Sylvie.

"We'll leave that for Inspector Seymour to decide," cautioned Bobo. "Now then, how do we go about finding the elusive Monsieur Lequet?"

"His last known address is as good as any place to start; perhaps the clerk in Ardennes can help us with that."

A couple of telephone calls later and they had an address, which soon saw Sylvie and Bobo heading for Ardennes at high speed; both curious why he had returned to the area where he lived as a young man. Knowing memories of the wartime occupation still lingered on; the return of a collaborator would not go unnoticed or challenged.

Tres Eglises isn't the prettiest of towns, but the loss of its traditional industries and consequent fall from grace have saved it from the urban blight; meaning the block of apartments which housed Monsieur Lequet was easily found. However, there was no reply when Sylvie rang his doorbell, having her question the neighbours if he was resident. One came out and looked down from the balcony, pointed to his car saying, he must be at home, because that man never walked anywhere. Suspicious, the two detectives returned to examine his apartment door, the presence of many flies and a faint, but odd smell, having them contact the local police for help.

They arrived and were soon convinced something was wrong, for having broken open the door the officers stopped and retreated, saying they had seen a suspicious package. With other residents evacuated from the building, it was an hour before an officer in charge of the bomb squad reported they had safely defused and removed an explosive device, from the apartment's kitchen. It had been positioned near the dead body of a man lying on the floor, set to be detonated by a motion sensor.

After examination by police officers it was confirmed the body was that of, Pierre Lequet, the apartment's resident. The body had bruising around the neck, wrists and ankles, with many stab wounds that left blood spatters all over the room and a large pool on the floor.

Sylvie and Bobo stayed in the town until receiving the pathology report, which confirmed what they already guessed; the victim had been gagged and bound before being systematically tortured for some time, then left to bleed out.

Bobo reported the facts back to Seymour, telling him a full report from the authorities would follow in due course. Then came some bad news for Bobo, now their enquiries in France were at an end, she should return to Swanscombe and report for duty the following day. Despite this meaning she would be home in time for some belated Christmas celebrations, the news led to a sombre mood, their return to Paris conducted without the normal chatter, plus there were tears from both as goodbyes were said at Charles de Gaulle airport, their short time together having made them firm friends.

CHAPTER FIFTY
'Pursuit'
Dorset, England, 1990

"News just in from Ardennes, Sir," said an excited Chalky. "The Gendarmerie confirmed what Bobo told us, plus a murder inquiry into the death has begun. The officer in charge said, his men found what they think says the word 'Dannet' scrawled on the floor by the victim; however, they have no idea who, or what it might mean. No witnesses had come forward saying they heard the gunshot, but several remember seeing a lone male drive off in an unknown car. Fortunately, a couple noted its Belgian registration, which was traced to a hire vehicle based at Brussels airport."

"Oh Lord, that leaves us with just one suspect, please tell me someone recognised Andrew Macintyre over there," pleaded Seymour.

"Not at the crime scene, but the hire car company clerk did," noted Chalky. "Plus, she noticed his airline ticket was to London/Gatwick."

"Not helpful, he could go just about anywhere from there, let's hope he favours staying at home."

Whilst waiting for replies from airlines operating from the airport, Chalky was tasked with finding out about the Macintyre family; though for once, the quest didn't take as long as expected.

"According to the 'Who's who'," Chalky told the assembled team, "Colin Andrew Macintyre was born in Aberdeen, Scotland, during nineteen-fifteen, was public school and university educated, before joining the Foreign Office in nineteen-thirty seven. His first posting as a junior diplomat was to Switzerland just months before the Second World War began, staying in Berne until the conflict ended. Post war, he served with distinction in Malaya, Kenya and South Africa before returning to London to work on Commonwealth matters."

"All very good, Chalky, but what relevance has this to our inquiry?" asked Seymour.

"I was coming to that, Sir," was his slightly annoyed reply. "Unfortunately Mister Macintyre died in nineteen-seventy-seven after suffering gunshot wounds during a grouse shoot near the family home in Aberdeenshire. There was a police investigation, but the coroner's verdict is recorded as 'accidental death'. He married Miss Muriel Coates in 'thirty eight and they had one son, Andrew, who was adopted in 'forty-four."

"Ah, I see where you are going with this, Chalky, continue,"

"The son, Andrew Malcolm Macintyre, had the same public school and university education, but joined the Army, becoming an officer in the Intelligence Corps, being based in West Germany. He resigned his commission after nine years and joined our M.I.6; so obviously the subsequent career remains undisclosed. At the present time he is unmarried."

"One wonders what happened when he found out about his adoption," mused Terry. "Also, did he attempt to find his birth mother?"

"Are you trying to build a case against this man, Sergeant?" queried Seymour.

"Yes, because he is now our only suspect, Sir: so is

this Andrew a crack shot and was he present at that fatal grouse shoot?" Terry asked.

"Yes to both, the Army had him classed as a marksman and he took part in the shoot where his father was killed." Chalky told him.

"The evidence is building up against him: a crack shot and intelligence operative, who is privy to information we can never see, whose father, birth mother and her killer have all died. Pretty damning I have to say, but one thing still bugs me, what is the motive behind all this?" Seymour admitted, while scribbling a note, which he handed to Chalky.

After glancing at the note, the DC nodded to his Inspector and left the incident room to find WPC Robbins; a quiet word having the two of them leave the police station and drive off.

CHAPTER FIFTY ONE
'To The North And Disaster'
Aberdeen, Scotland, 1990

After packing their cases, Chalky and Joy had driven off going north, both fully recovered from their respective Christmas celebrations, remembering to monitor whether they were being followed; until reaching Newcastle by dusk, where they stayed overnight. Booked in at a motel, they worked on their plan for the next day over dinner; deciding to start off early, praying that bad weather wouldn't delay their progress along roads neither of them had travelled before.

Despite grey skies, heavy rain and high winds along the way, it was just getting dark when they eventually arrived in Aberdeen, time enough to liaise with the local police; agreeing they would begin their investigations the next day.

Up bright and early, they were provided with a local constable as their guide; who confirmed that the original family home had been sold on by Andrew after his father's death, but Muriel Macintyre had moved to and was still resident in Dyce, near the airport. Meanwhile, Seymour had contacted a friend in London to conduct a discreet stake out of Macintyre's rented home in Bayswater; though it was soon evident the adopted son wasn't there. Nor was he visible in or around the Aberdeen area, so while the search was quietly spread further afield; Chalky telephoned Seymour from a public call box telling him of the situation.

"Oh, my idea of Mister Macintyre running for home and familiar territory hasn't worked out very well; we have him on camera passing through Gatwick, but where he went from there is anyone's guess."

"In that case would it be advisable to question Mrs Macintyre about her son's whereabouts, she might know of a place he favours?" asked Chalky.

"Well okay, but play it by ear and question everything she says; you know as well as I do, mothers can be overly protective when it concerns their own."

"Will do, Sir, 'bye."

Returning to the police station, he told Joy and their local man what he proposed, then they left driving off in the direction of Dyce. Following directions it led to a well presented bungalow whose front garden was now just bare grass and evergreen shrubs, any flowers having succumbed in the recent cold weather. Their guide knocked on the door and introduced everyone to the grey haired lady who answered it, asking if she was willing to answer some questions they had. She looked them up and down then let them in, having all three sat down in her lounge.

"Well, I'm all ears, what is it you want?" Muriel Macintyre asked politely.

"We are here at the behest of colleagues in France investigating a murder; one Pierre Lequet was murdered in his own home by a man now identified as your son..."

"You mean my adopted son," she shot back. "I knew that little fool would never amount to anything, creeping around pretending to be some kind of a secret agent."

"According to our information, Madame, he does still work for the Intelligence service of the United Kingdom," Chalky reminded her. "So he could well be a spy."

"More fool them; perhaps they should ask who he is spying for?"

"Whoa, this has no bearing on our inquiry," he ordered. "Let's get back to the reason for our visit, what we would like to know is, have you any idea of where he might be now, or any place he favours?"

"Anywhere wild, he liked hunting and roaming around the Highlands in his younger days; or the Hartz mountains when he was in Germany. I don't know about recent times, we haven't spoken since his father's funeral."

"Thank you, just one more thing, do you have any guns in this house?"

"Yes, there's my husband's old shotgun and his service revolver; before you ask, I have licences for them."

"May we see both, please?" had her take them to a utility room and unlock a metal cupboard, where they checked out the double barrelled, twelve bore shotgun, noting there was plenty of spare boxes of ammunition in there as well. Satisfied, the older lady led them to her bedroom, where she opened a bedside cabinet drawer and rummaged around.

"Well, it was in here, I only cleaned it last week..."

"And now it's pointing right at you," came a male voice behind them. "Please, no silly moves by anyone, they could be your last."

"Don't be so bloody stupid, Andrew, put that thing down and ...," her step forward ended with a loud gunshot, having her jolt backwards into a wardrobe and slide to the floor. Joy couldn't stop herself; she dropped down to help Muriel Macintyre, only to hear another gunshot, feel terrible pain then everything going black.

"You, find some cord and tie up our uniformed friend here," came as a warm gun barrel was pressed into Chalky's back, "and make sure the bonds are tight."

The three of them back tracked to the utility room where Chalky found a length of washing line, tying up the hands and feet of the constable with it. After checking his handiwork, Andrew Macintyre hurried him to the car, where pushed into its driving seat, Chalky drove off following his instructions.

The journey lasted a bare ten minutes, before they reached a secluded spot, abandoning his car for the Land Rover parked alongside them. As before Chalky drove, taking instructions from his gun wielding companion, who had him hurtling along a series of narrow roads as they climbed ever higher towards the swirling grey clouds and rain. Up until now Chalky had stayed quiet, wondering if he could start a conversation with his abductor, eventually venturing to speak.

"Excuse me, Andrew, but I am confused by all this, what did you hope to gain by your actions at the bungalow; you must realise it can only end in more tragedy?"

"What's more tragic than finding out your real mother, a French killer for hire, no less, had abandoned you days after your birth," he said quietly. "No attempt to find me was ever carried out, but after many years of searching, when I eventually discovered she was alive and living in England, that bastard Lequet killed her before I had a chance to confront my mother."

"This we already know, Andrew; I sympathise, it's been a long, sad history of circumstance and consequences for her and you, but it can't excuse your recent actions."

"There you go again Mister Policeman, quoting the law; why must the ordinary individual always pay for his sins, whilst the rich, elite and politicians are allowed to commit mass murder with impunity?" his voice almost inaudible now, as the downpour of rain beat a tattoo on their vehicle's bodywork. The difficult conditions had Chalky fall silent again, concentrating even more when directed onto a dirt track, its slippery surface having him engage all wheel drive to maintain any forward motion. Thirty minutes of this and temperatures had dropped further, the rain changed to snow, which fell at such a rate the track ahead was soon barely visible. The vehicle's engine had growled on remorselessly, though its windscreen wipers now gave mere seconds of clear view ahead, making this already hazardous journey even more so.

"This is getting ridiculous," complained Chalky as they slithered blindly over the rocky ground, "I'll end up killing us both at this rate."

"Don't be such a sissy, man," came the reply, "A few more minutes and we arrive at our shelter for tonight."

As promised, the arrival came sooner than expected, where thanking God for their survival, Chalky finally brought the Land Rover to a halt underneath a large rocky outcrop, to be pushed out of the vehicle and into a wooden hut.

"Get a fire going," were his orders, as the entrance was locked behind him. Peering into the gloom he saw six bunk beds, a small table, some chairs and an old fashioned, metal stove. Alongside this was a stack of firewood and a small box, which contained firelighters plus a means of ignition. By the time Andrew reappeared, there was a fire warming the dank atmosphere, having him grunt in approval.

"So, what happens now?" Chalky asked cautiously, beginning to shiver.

"I would have thought that was blindingly obvious, young man," he replied. "We stay here until the weather allows us to continue."

"I didn't mean that, where are we heading for?" Chalky insisted.

"That's for me to know and you to guess; don't panic, I have no plans to kill you, so just behave."

"What is this place?" he asked looking around, his shivers continuing despite the fire's increasing warmth.

"It's a mountain refuge for climbers caught out by bad weather," Macintyre told him, "but this one hasn't been used for years."

"Look, I'm sorry, but I'd like to know; with your successful career now in ruins, how have things ended up like this for you?"

"Before I tell you have a swig of this, I can't concentrate with you sat there shaking away," a bottle passed over with the reply. Chalky's first gulp of the whisky had him gag, but its warmth spread around his body subduing the shivers.

"Well," Macintyre began, "I suppose it all started on being told that Muriel wasn't my real mother, plus a warning that trying to find this lady could only lead to more heartache. However, there was no way to just forget about her: but, from then on other things in life took precedence, my education and the Army years had me totally absorbed, so nothing was done until I returned to civilian life." He paused, as if thinking back to that time.

"The impetus came after joining the secret service," he eventually continued, "where a job liaising with our French counterparts revealed my mother's history in their wartime Resistance movement and later service for the country. This restarted my quest to find and confront Marie Montagne; though I have to say the widely publicised career in the fashion world and reports of her death only served to confuse the issue. Years later, an old university chum who was an operative in West Berlin contacted me, saying a Marie Bergamont was being used by his boss, Connel Dannet. His description of this Marie tallied with my Marie, so I concluded they were one and the same person; but finding out where she lived proved impossible, for nothing was written down and only Dannet had that information."

He stopped talking and frowned, as if the next part was particularly distasteful to him, only talking again after Chalky had put some more wood on the fire.

"Somehow, my father found out or was told about my continuing search for Marie, which led to a blazing row on the afternoon before his death," he recalled tiredly. "When, as you no doubt know, I was considered a prime suspect after the shooting. Though quite rightly found innocent of any wrongdoing, Muriel remained adamant my obsession with Marie was somehow the cause of her husband's death, so I left after sorting out his affairs, never to return until now. My quest almost ended in 'eighty-four when Dannet was returned to England and retired, because there was no mention of Marie in Berlin from then on. It wasn't until 'eighty-eight that a report ended up on my desk, a red starred one, indicating there could be a problem at one of our 'secure locations', Dolhurst in Dorset. Reading it, the name, Marie Angelique Bergamont, stood out; at last, could I finally meet up with my real mother?" Macintyre stopped there to berate Chalky, who was shivering nonstop again; telling him to take another swig from the whisky bottle.

 "The answer is no, for events in Germany had me returned to Berlin, where I stayed long after the Wall came down," he stated. "Our complete intelligence apparatus there had to be reorganised, a 24/7 project, which only finished in the summer of this year. Then, another blow, returning to London a friend advised me that my mother was terminally ill; so when the debriefing was completed, I immediately left for Dorset. During that journey, all thoughts were jumbled and confused, would it be pent up anger or joy at meeting after so long; or just relief that it happened before the inevitable. No, I eventually decided; just keep an open mind about the meeting. Parking my car before reaching the village, I passed a foreign vehicle, something having me commit its registration and garage name to memory. Approaching my mother's cottage, there was the subdued stutter of a sub machine gun; then moments later, I nearly came face to face with a black clad figure carrying a bag, as he hurried away. Rushing to the open front door and peering inside, there was my mother lying on the floor, her small body a mess of blood and gore. Turning away in blind fury, to realise all those years devoted to finding her had ended in a mere glance, I saw red and swore the perpetrator would suffer horribly for this deed; my only thought being, to wreak revenge, a terrible revenge. Closing the door and fleeing to my car, I noted the other one had also departed; so a trip to France was required to sort out the whys and wherefores of this murderous act."

A half asleep Chalky looked at Macintyre, whose whole demeanour now seemed relaxed, wondering if their conversation could be used in evidence against him.

"I presume you know what happened to Pierre Lequet," Macintyre stated loudly, receiving a nod. "But have you guessed, or do you know who told him where my mother lived?"

"There must be several people who knew, the most obvious being, this Mister Dannet," considered Chalky, who was beginning to shiver again.

"Well done, young man, she was condemned by the very person who recruited and trusted her."

"Oh Christ, you haven't killed him as well, have you?" he muttered lamely.

There was no reply, just a proffered whisky bottle to cure his shivers, while Macintyre added more wood to the fire; then consulted his watch.

"Right, it's time to make ourselves comfortable for the night; these blankets may smell bad but at least they will keep us warm."

Chalky didn't reply, just wrapped himself up, lay on a bunk bed nearest the fire, now more interested in this source of warmth than worrying about his present situation, to quickly fall asleep.

Unsurprisingly, it was a gnawing chill that woke him, to discover the fire was almost out and his captor missing; feeling disorientated, it took some time to restore the fire; then stagger outside to discover the Land Rover had also vanished. This extreme cold, high winds and snowfall soon had him weaving a way back inside the hut, where he sat down trying to concentrate on his situation. The muddled brain finally registered his abductor had left, intent on eliminating one final victim, Connel Dannet. Oh bugger, he thought, Inspector Seymour, your plan to arrest Andrew Macintyre has blown up in our faces! Not only that his immediate future looked bleak, for having no idea where he was, while lacking food and drink or any means of communication, what could be done? Before anything came to mind, an overpowering weariness overcame the confused thoughts, having him curl up on the bunk bed and fall asleep.

CHAPTER FIFTY TWO
'Good And Bad News, Plus A Plan'
Dorset, England, 1990

Seymour's face turned almost white as he listened intently to the telephone call from Scotland, others in the incident room realising it was bad news when they heard the exclamations of 'Oh God no' and 'not more' coming from his office. When he replaced the receiver, there was a pause before he hurried out to stand before them.

"Right people, things have gone very wrong up there in Aberdeen, Mrs Muriel Macintyre has been shot dead by her adopted son, WPC Robbins is in intensive care with gunshot wounds, while DC White has been abducted at gunpoint by the killer. A local Constable who was with them has been treated for minor injuries, though he has given valuable information to the armed search party regarding where the killer might be heading. At present, freezing temperatures, snow showers and gale force winds on high ground have brought the search to a halt; it will be resumed when the weather clears. Terry, you are in charge for now, so make sure the families are informed of what has happened; meanwhile, I have a plane to catch."

There were hurried greetings on his arrival at Aberdeen, because the weather had at last changed for the better, so their search had been resumed, with a helicopter available for transporting people to distant or inaccessible places. Macintyre's hire car had been found abandoned at a parking spot on the way to the mountains, so what form of transport he had now was unknown. There was no news of DC White, but until it was proved otherwise, the searchers were assuming he was still with his abductor.

Seymour went to the hospital hoping to see WPC Robbins, but doctors insisted there would be no visitors, telling him they successfully operated on her to repair the gunshot damage. She was now in a 'serious but stable' condition and would remain in intensive care until they saw positive signs of recovery; while refusing to speculate when that might be.

He retreated and joined the police search party, who, with the assistance of a local mountain rescue team, were now climbing the steeper slopes. It was hard and unrewarding work for him, because the rugged surroundings looked as if they had never seen a human being in centuries, so he was relieved when the senior officers called in the helicopter. It clattered overhead some twenty minutes later and headed for the higher reaches to begin its search pattern, while those on the ground plodded on.

It was late afternoon before they received a message from the air, reporting smoke had been seen and on their reaching the source, a person appeared waving slowly at them. However, with no safe landing place available nearby, his location was relayed to the searchers; while a survival pack had been dropped to the man, because he definitely wasn't dressed for the weather. Convinced this was Chalky, Seymour gamely tried to stay with those heading for the given location; though it soon became clear locals were much fitter and accustomed to this kind of hike.

It was getting dark by the time their helicopter guided the mountain rescue group to this lone man, who they discovered was acting strangely, their medic soon ascertaining he was still suffering from a drug mixed in the whisky this 'Andrew' gave him. Having been airlifted away by helicopter to hospital by the time Seymour arrived at the scene, he was told his DC White kept muttering, 'Macintyre, kill Dannet, MI6.'

The message was all too clear to him, but with the restrictions placed on his inquiry, how could his team discover Mister Dannet's address before it was too late? After arranging for his request to be relayed to Dorset, Seymour sat back to realise he was stuck up this mountain until dawn; a frustration that would make a good night's rest impossible.

Up before dawn, he was willing the rest to join him and set off downhill at a trot; but was soon overtaken by the experienced mountaineering team, who guided him to their transport. Coming down from that highest vehicle access point was a slow and uncomfortable ride, as the Land Rover navigated its way along the rocky tracks until, at long last, they reached a tarmac road.

Dropped off at the hospital in Aberdeen, he found that Chalky was uninjured and none the worse for his night in the mountain; but was now sedated until effects from the opiate he was given had left his system. However, before being put to sleep, he managed to tell the doctor about Macintyre's vehicle and registration; again stating he was convinced his abductor was intent on killing Connel Dannet.

A relieved, but worried Seymour entered the local

police station, knowing the inquiry had come to an unsatisfactory end, with his main suspect now dead. Furthermore, Lequet's murder had the French examining magistrate applying to extradite Macintyre, while his subsequent slayings also had the Scottish Constabulary after him; creating a right royal mess. Nevertheless, complications aside, he was determined to see this case to a satisfactory conclusion; telling the Scots team about restrictions posed by the Secret Service, while offering to work in conjunction with them, by immediately returning south to find Dannet before Macintyre got to him.

Knowing that obtaining permission to operate in a different country would take time and equally unhappy about the possibility of having their multiple murder case closed down by London, they readily agreed; Seymour was found a seat on the next flight to Bristol.

Meanwhile, DS Morton was in a cold and windswept Swanscombe, having called on Bob Watts to ask if Marie had ever mentioned where a Mister Dannet lived. The answer was negative, for he had never heard of this man; only that the person who arranged her settlement in England must have lived within an hour's drive. This was because he had also mentioned about retirement and wanting to be home before nightfall. Well, breathed Terry, it's better than nothing; deciding to draw a circle on a map around Marie's home, to where he considered the limit of one hour's driving would be.

It turned out to cover a large area, so he ignored the cities and all towns, large or small, concentrating on all hidden away places like Dolhurst. His search left him with seven possible sites, more than there were people available to discreetly check them out; not helpful, for he realised they might arrive too late to stop yet another death.

 Risking all; he asked for three uniformed police officers to volunteer and help them trace an armed and dangerous individual. Those who did were told to change into ordinary clothing; then drive their own cars to one of the selected sites, to ask about their old friend, Connel. If found, they must contact Terry immediately, then persuade this elderly man to leave with them; meanwhile, all the other cars would converge on the site, await developments and be ready to block off all likely escape routes. There were flaws in all this, facts which had Terry praying Dannet and Macintyre wouldn't meet before they had identified the older man; for, as yet, no one knew what he looked like. Conversely, everyone involved had a likeness of Macintyre with them, but confronting him without an armed response team present might result in more deaths.

 Collecting Seymour from a foggy Bristol airport, Terry ordered the police driver take them to the nearest site at all speed, so, as they hurtled past the slower traffic with lights flashing and siren wailing, his Inspector was told of what had been arranged.

 "Good grief, Terry, you've pushed it to the limit," he said, "but I agree, what else can we do, without having our Security types closing us down. Let's hope the Armed Response team can arrive by the vital moment." With that he fell silent, thinking of various scenarios which might result in an arrest without any violence; knowing only too well that the best laid plans could and did go awry.

There were no lights or siren to disturb the peace of the first village they visited; their undercover policeman reporting that the locals and pub landlord had never heard of any 'Connel' or 'Dannet'.

"Do you realise, Terry, this man's unusual name is about the only thing in our favour," commented Seymour. "Hopefully everyone who has heard it will remember what the person looked like."

There was no joy at the next two sites they visited; but on the way to Terry's fourth, their driver reported they had a tail. This blue car with a woman driver; had followed their every move since they left the last site.

"Okay, do a check on its registration," ordered the Inspector, "while we try a short diversion to see what happens."

The blue car was nowhere to be seen when the police car returned to its intended route; while their check had revealed the blue car's legal owner was a Mrs Sandra Deedes of Bayswater, London. Suspicions forgotten, they continued on heading for Manor Oak, a village situated in the middle of a large wooded area. Terry found its narrow access road eerily similar to Dolhurst's, suggesting that on arrival, they should park their police car somewhere out of sight. This was done, along with sending an urgent radio message.

"You're convinced this is where Dannet lives?" queried Seymour, looking around as they walked into this quiet village, past several neatly presented houses and it's solitary facility, a pub, to a small green area at the centre. "Okay, now where is your undercover man?"

"Behind you, Sir, didn't you get my message?" the soft voice asked with menace. "There are people watching, so let's greet as friends; then I'll take you to Mister Dannet's house."

They did as he asked, hiding their surprise upon recognising who it was; then the three of them strode off towards an ancient thatched house, conveniently situated to give good views of the approach road.

CHAPTER FIFTY THREE
'Explanations And End Game'
Devon, England, 1991

A gun appeared as they entered the house to see a grey haired, elderly man gagged and bound to a dining table chair, Seymour and Morton being ordered to sit on a nearby sofa.

"Now then, before you sits Mister Connel Dannet, a man who considers his cosy existence and pension more important than another person's life," stated Macintyre, removing the gag. "It was he who was ordered to inform the Nazi collaborator Lequet where my mother lived, thereby condemning her to death."

"Stop right there, dear boy, you know as well as I, orders are orders, anyway your mother was already terminally ill with cancer," Dannet replied.

"True, but you knew of my search, yet even after having arranged her safe haven in England and your retirement, I was never informed of where that was."

"Firstly, there is no such thing as retiring from the Intelligence game," was his answer. "Secondly, don't act naive in front of these policemen, as a member of the 'firm', you know damn well it's a tightly controlled existence, where our masters require you to lie, confuse, steal, or even kill to obtain what they need; saying no is not an option."

"Nevertheless, that doesn't excuse your betrayal," Macintyre said in a raised voice. "London's games had my mother murdered, which has led to more unnecessary deaths, so I suggest you also prepare yourself for the ultimate sacrifice."

"So be it, I'm an old man; my passing will change nothing."

Next moment the back door crashed open, as a smartly dressed lady ran through the house.

"Come on, Andrew, we have to leave, now!" she gasped at Macintyre, "there's armed police entering the village."

"And so it ends," he concluded, as Sandra Deedes dragged him towards the open door; but Morton's quick lunge forward had the chair and Dannet on the floor, meaning the bullet intended for him merely damaged contents of a nearby wooden cabinet. Hardly had the chair been put upright and Dannet untied, when armed police burst through the front door pointing guns at them. When allowed to explain themselves, they left with all but one, who was told to guard Dannet and prevent him from communicating with anybody.

Seymour was still hurrying through the house's back garden when a loud explosion had him thrown to the ground, covered in wood and glass fragments; while smoke billowed from the smashed door and windows.

"Oh please God, not more victims," he muttered to himself. "How many more have to die because of one unnecessary murder." Looking up, he saw his Sergeant running back towards the house.

"All okay, just a few cuts and bruises," he shouted to him. "I'll sort this mess out; you just get that bastard for me, but I want him alive."

Confronted with cold, wet and dense woodland, the police and Morton had no choice but to spread out and look for the trail their fleeing pair left, something which wasted precious time until it was eventually discovered. With his bulky equipment being torn at by twigs and thorn bushes, their eagle-eyed leader ran on doggedly following the footprints, until a glimpse of blue had him stop briefly; signalling the rest to spread out ready for an ambush. Moving forward as quickly and quietly as possible, the plan was foiled when this car took off down a firebreak, only slithering to a halt when its tyres were punctured by their rifle fire.

The male passenger jumped out, his gun moving around in search of a target, as shouts for his surrender echoed amongst the trees. Meanwhile, the female driver had alighted, hands held high as she encouraged him to do likewise; but an unusual noise spooked Macintyre, who turned round and fired blindly. The already agitated wood pigeons flapped noisily around in renewed distress as Sandra Deedes fell, wounded by a gunshot to her head. On realising what he had done Macintyre looked over at the body, allowing a police marksman's shot to disable his right arm, the pistol falling onto muddy ground. Within seconds he was pinned down, disarmed and handcuffed by the fast moving officers; while another examining Mrs Deedes looked up and shook his head at Morton. His dismay was cut short when another car appeared; this time containing four police officers recently arrived from Aberdeen, who took over control from Morton and formally arrested the prisoner.

While they awaited a tow truck, Seymour arrived, saying the two in the house were badly injured, but alive, awaiting an ambulance; while the Fire Brigade were now making Dannet's house safe, ready for a pathology unit to conduct their examination. With another ambulance on its way to this location, his handover was completed; though he quietly prayed there would be no backlash from London, especially as the Metropolitan police would have to investigate Mrs Deedes involvement in all this.

With Macintyre taken to hospital for treatment and their female victim to its pathology department, their Scottish colleagues bade them farewell; leaving Morton to recall the other officers sent to his selected sites, including the one found uninjured, but bound and gagged in an upstairs room of Dannet's home.

Sat comfortably in the back of a police car for the journey back to Dorset, Seymour examined his overcoat, wondering what his wife would have to say about the irreparable damage, let alone the various cuts and bruises he sported.

"Oh my Lord," he suddenly remembered, "with all that has happened recently, I forgot to ask about DS White and WPC Robbins, please tell me it's good news."

"Panic not, Sir, Chalky has been discharged from hospital and is on his way back home," Morton informed him. "While Joy has been removed from Intense Care, now her recovery is on track; though after that there will be more tests, physiotherapy, et cetera, to complete before she can return home."

This had the Inspector smile with relief, though when the police car passed a large public house, its frontage still strung with one large gaudy sign, coloured lights and partially deflated balloons, his expression changed to a worried frown.

"Oh dear, my homecoming will be no happy reunion with the family," Morton was told. "I promised they were to enjoy a special New Year's Eve party in Exeter; the girls will have been all dressed up, but left with nowhere to go; here's hoping our conversation remains civil. Not only that, first thing tomorrow morning, I foresee Superintendent Wallis having me in his office; wanting a detailed explanation of this recent fracas."

"Never mind Sir, remember, your efforts have bought three murder inquiries to successful conclusions; Happy New Year!"

THE END

Acknowledgements

A special mention for members of 'Writers Ink' for their advice and guidance, special thanks to Janette Davies for her assistance and knowledge during the publication process.

Previous Work by the Author

Novels

>The Accountant
>Jupiter's Revenge
>The Vienna Connection
>Out of the Shadows

Short Story Compilation

>Déjà vu!

Anthologies (contributing author)

>Talk of the Towns.
>Leaping into Christmas.
>Food, glorious Food.
>Fifty by Fifty.
>Des Res?

About the Author

Nigel Grundey was born in Warwickshire, but brought up in Kent.

He first qualified as a mechanical engineer; however, at age twenty one he joined H.M. Forces, serving in the Far East and West Germany as an aircraft engineer.

Unsure of what to do next, a stint in college followed, furthering his qualifications.

"You do realise there is a war going on out there!" is not the normal opening line of a job interview; but it led to nearly thirty years with the same company, working with aircraft in the Middle East and U.K.

Always a voracious reader, he didn't consider writing until retirement, but is delighted that many of his stories have now been published.

Never a fan of cold weather, he now lives in Southern Spain.

www.ingramcontent.com/pod-product-compliance
Lightning Source LLC
Chambersburg PA
CBHW061241120726
48001CB00001B/86